I0452242

Look for More Titles by Cassandra Chandler

Other Works
CRAFTING A WRITER'S LIFE: Building a Foundation

Coming Soon

The Blades of Janus
PERIHELION

The Department of Homeworld Security
Nothing to Declare

Entry Visa

The Department of Homeworld Security
Book Five

Cassandra Chandler

Copyright Page

You are a good person! You know that stealing is wrong. Remember, ebooks can't be shared or given away. It's against copyright law. So don't download books you haven't paid for or upload books in ways other people can access for free. That would be stealing. And you're better than that.

This book is pure fiction. All characters, places, names, and events are products of the author's imagination or used solely in a fictitious manner. Any resemblance to any people, places, things, or events that have ever existed or will ever exist is entirely coincidental.

Entry Visa
The Department of Homeworld Security, Book Five
Copyright © 2016 by Cassandra Chandler
Print ISBN: 978-1-945702-36-5
Digital ISBN: 978-1-945702-24-2

All Rights Reserved. No part of this book may be used, transmitted, or reproduced in any manner or form without written permission from the author, except for brief quotations used in critical articles and reviews.

First eBook edition: July 2017
First print edition: December 2018
10 9 8 7 6 5 4 3 2 1

cassandra-chandler.com
P.O. Box 91
Mission, Kansas 66201

Dedication

For my book club—thanks for waiting.

Don't miss out on any of the alien action.
Subscribe to Cassandra Chandler's newsletter at
cassandra-chandler.com!

Prologue

"A Homeworld Holiday"

Christmas Eve

"Who in their right mind spends two hours tracking down a fruitcake on Christmas Eve?" Henry spoke under his breath, even though no one was nearby. "Oh yeah. I forgot. I'm not in my right mind."

He ran his hand through his hair, knowing it would make his brown curls stand on end and not caring. Finding an open store was something of a miracle. Now if only it had what he needed to fulfill his family's tradition—even though his family didn't exist anymore.

He shook his head, as if the movement could keep the dark thoughts from taking root in his mind.

There were beautiful lights all around him. He focused on the colorful strands, looking at the lavishly decorated holiday aisle. His gaze landed on a single brick of fruitcake sitting in a large display basket.

"Bingo!"

He practically leapt at it, his fingers closing over the prize just as another hand reached for it. Reflexively, he pulled back, cradling the fruitcake against his chest.

His heart beat fast, his hindbrain reminding him of close calls he'd had with rattlesnakes and other bitey animals in the woods. But it was winter, and the snakes were all hibernating. Plus, he was back in civilization surrounded by people. One of whom he'd probably just offended.

"Sorry, I..." His words stuck in his throat.

He was staring into the biggest, deepest blue eyes he'd ever seen. They were open wide, the woman's lips parted and her dark eyebrows hitched up her forehead. The red and green stocking cap she wore couldn't quite hide the blonde hair that stuck out from underneath it, barely brushing her shoulders.

She was almost as tall as him, which put her at nearly six feet. With the impossibly perfect symmetry of her features, she could easily be some sort of supermodel. Except for her quirky, definitely not mainstream fashion-sense.

She was wearing jeans and an incredibly ugly sweater under an overstuffed coat. He could make out antlers on what was probably supposed to be a moose. It was hard to look at the pattern of her sweater with all the different colors on it fighting for his attention—or maybe trying to blind him.

"Wow," he said. "I mean, 'hi'. And this is the last fruitcake. You should have it. Here."

Her lips curved into a huge smile as he offered it to her. Her front two teeth stuck out just the tiniest bit more than the others. It was adorable.

She shook her head. "No, it's yours."

"But there aren't any more." He looked back in the basket, as if he might have missed one in the obviously empty container.

She laughed. Henry felt color flood his cheeks at the sound.

"I'll survive," she said.

"Coffee can help with that." He would absolutely need some to make the drive back to his parents' cabin. *His* cabin now.

"Coffee?" One eyebrow arced and her smile turned into a smirk.

"It's a hot beverage that helps you stay awake. Or so I've heard."

She laughed again, even though his joke was utterly lame. Her smile broadened.

"Let me get you a cup. Since you're being so gracious about the fruitcake."

What was he doing? It had been a while since he'd spoken to anyone...other than himself. And here he was asking out a total stranger. An absolutely gorgeous stranger.

Plus, it was Christmas Eve. She had to have better things to do than hang out with an itinerant, aspiring cryptozoologist.

But she shrugged and said, "Okay."

"Okay?" His forehead nearly cramped from his eyebrows spiking up. He cleared his throat and forced his expression into the closest thing to neutrality he could manage. "Okay."

They walked to the cashier together, and she watched with open curiosity as he paid. Strangely, it reminded him of his biology classes—how they'd been taught to observe wildlife. He shook away the thought as absurd, and vowed to never be away from civilization for that many weeks again.

"Shall we?" He gestured to the door.

"We shall."

He laughed as he followed her into the snowy night.

The sidewalks were clear, but drifts lined the street and hugged the walls where the snow had been pushed away. Wreaths and bright snowflake decorations made of lights alternated on the streetlamps over their heads.

"I'm Henry, by the way."

"Henry." She nodded, then held out her hand to him. "I'm Vay."

He slipped the fruitcake into his coat pocket and shook her hand. "Vay? That's an unusual name."

She shrugged, still pumping his hand up and down. "You're the first 'Henry' I've met."

"Really? I always thought it was a ridiculously common name."

"Depends on where you're from."

"Do they shake hands this long on your homeworld?"

She gasped and pulled her hand back like he'd stung her.

"I'm sorry," he said. "That was just my pathetic attempt at humor."

"Oh. A joke."

He tried to recover and figure out what had set her off. If nerd humor wasn't her thing, getting coffee with him was going to be an ordeal for her.

"I guess I should also mention that I'm kind of a huge nerd. I make obscure science fiction references and tell weird jokes that probably only I find funny." Although, she'd laughed at a couple already. That was part of why he'd had the courage to ask her for coffee.

"I see. I have a friend like that. Do you also make puns?"

"'Make puns'?" He laughed at her odd word choice. "Yes, I do make Earth human puns."

She snorted and stuck her hands in her pockets, her smile returning. "Well, where do you get this Earth human coffee of which you speak?"

"That would be at the all night diner. We have many on

our planet." He started walking again, his pace picking up as she fell in step beside him. When they reached the door, he held it open for her and said, "Welcome."

She ducked into the warmth and light of the restaurant, still smiling at him. Another Christmas miracle.

Her eyes broadened as she looked around, taking in the ceiling tiles, grubby carpet, booths, and long bar that ran along the side of the space. A bedraggled Christmas tree stood nearby, covered in lights and ornaments that looked like they were homemade. Vay walked over to it with a rapt expression on her face.

"Would you like to sit here?" He gestured to the booth next to the tree—specifically to the seat that would let her stare at it while they had their coffee.

"Is it okay?"

"Sure."

They slid into their booths, staring at each other. He wasn't sure how such a beautiful woman managed a goofy smile, but he was pretty sure his matched.

A waitress showed up with two cups of coffee and a carafe. "You want something from the kitchen?"

"I'm good," Henry said. He looked over at Vay. "You?"

"This is fine, thank you." She smiled at the waitress as the woman walked away, then leaned over her coffee and inhaled deeply, her eyes closing briefly. "This smells amazing."

"Diners often have the best coffee."

He picked up some sugar packets and flicked them back and forth to get all the granules in the bottom, then tore them open. Vay watched with that same keen interest as she'd had at the store, then followed his example. She waited for him to pour them in his coffee before doing the same, and even picked up her spoon after he did. It was like watching a time-delay alternate reality mirror.

Why was she mimicking him, though? It was almost as if she'd never made herself a cup of coffee before. He tested the thought, watching her as he picked up some creamers and poured them into his coffee. Sure enough, she did the same.

There were several types of hot sauce on the table. He picked one up and shook it, pretending to prepare it for his drink.

She looked at the bottles, then grabbed one that resembled his.

"Okay, hold on a minute." He put the hot sauce back in place. "You've had coffee before, right?"

Her eyes grew wide again and her mouth dropped open. "Uh…"

"You've never had coffee?"

She set down the bottle and wiped her hands on her jeans. "Maybe this wasn't such a good idea."

She slid toward the edge of the booth seat, setting her hand on the table as she prepared to leave. Henry reached out and grabbed it. She stared at his hand on hers, as if that was yet another thing that was new to her.

"Wait." His heart was pounding.

He didn't want to be alone. Not tonight. And even though Vay was turning out to be…really weird company, he liked her. She laughed at his jokes, and had a kind of vulnerability about her that made him want to help her, even though she didn't seem to need it.

"Please stay," he said.

She took a deep breath, then nodded and slid back onto the seat. She turned her hand over in his and held on.

"Thank you," he said.

Her smile was more hesitant. "I don't really know much about this area. I saw the lights and…I just had to stop by and see what it was all about."

"You're from someplace that doesn't have Christmas?"

The drawn expression returned to her face, and her fingers tightened on his hand. It wasn't too strange to think of her not celebrating the holiday, but she seemed completely ignorant about it. He squeezed back, trying to find a way to put her at ease.

"Right," he said. "I forgot for a moment that the ways of my homeworld are alien to you."

She cast another suspicious look at him. He smiled, hoping to draw on the common sense of humor they seemed to share.

"I mean, even on Earth, Christmas is one holiday

among many," he said. "There are tons of holidays around this time of year that I know nothing about. I'm just following my family's traditions."

A sharp stab of pain passed through his heart and his vision blurred for a moment. Vay tightened her grip on his hand again. She must have noticed.

"My friend who plays with words like you do is visiting her family. I thought she was celebrating someone's...'birthday'?" Vay said the word as if she was unsure of herself—or uncertain of its meaning. "Now I wonder if I misunderstood her."

"Why?" His heart felt tight. He was getting better at reining in his emotions, even if his imagination was playing tricks on him. It had to be. Who didn't know about birthdays?

Vay smiled and shook her head. "She spoke of celebrating Hana...something. Hana is a common name where I'm from."

"Hanukkah," Henry said. "She was probably talking about Hanukkah. It's another holiday celebrated around this time of year. We Earthlings are a diverse bunch."

Vay smiled at him, as if she really enjoyed playing along with his joke. "The commonalities are stronger, from what I've observed. Otherwise, you would have destroyed each other long ago."

"Oh, really?" He took a sip of his coffee, daring to rub his thumb over the backs of her fingers.

A flush rose to her cheeks and she stared at their entwined hands. She cleared her throat and glanced at him briefly, then turned to look out the window.

"You join together with your families in the darkest, coldest part of the year. You celebrate with lights and... proximity." She looked back at their hands. "Lights in darkness. Togetherness in the cold. As a...space-faring wanderer, that is something I can understand."

Her smile broadened again. Henry's stomach was full of butterflies.

Not just playing along—she was expanding on the game.

"Where have you been all my life?" The words slipped out before he could stop himself.

"Lots of places. Too many." She shook her head and said, "And unfortunately, I need to get back."

"So soon?"

"My ride is waiting for me."

"Oh."

"But thank you for the coffee." She pulled her hand from his, picking up the mug and taking a sip. Her eyes widened and she made a terrible face, sticking out her tongue and scrunching her eyes shut. "Cygnus-X, this is terrible!"

Henry busted out laughing. Vay kept shaking her head and even wiped her tongue on her coat sleeve. That only made him laugh harder.

"Sorry," he managed, though tears were streaming down his face. "I know I shouldn't laugh."

"How do you drink this vile substance?"

"It's an acquired taste, I guess. Some people don't like it."

"I'm among their number." She gave her head one last shake, wiping her tongue on the roof of her mouth. "I do appreciate you procuring it for me."

He wiped his eyes dry, regaining control. "Any time. In fact, I would love to do this again. Only with a substance less vile."

She grinned at him. "I would like that, too."

Henry pulled out a pen and wrote his number on a napkin, then handed it to her. "Next time your travels bring you near, give me a call."

She picked up the paper and stared at the numbers, then folded it and tucked it inside her coat. "If it is at all in my power, I will."

Henry downed his coffee while Vay made yuck noises and smiled at him. He managed not to choke laughing. He put enough money on the table to cover their drinks and give the waitress a really nice tip.

They slid from the booth and stood. Wherever Vay was from, they had differing ideas of personal space. She was only inches away, smiling up at him.

"I know you're new to the ways of our Earthling holidays, but there's another fairly common thread that runs through most of them this time of year," Henry said.

"What's that?"

"Gifts." He picked up one of her hands, then pulled out the fruitcake and placed it in her grasp.

"But you wanted this."

"Honestly, I don't even like fruitcake. I was just trying to hold on to..." He shook his head. "Something that's passed. I want you to have it."

"I have nothing to give you in return."

"You gave me your company. Your time. And at this moment, that is worth more to me than I can say."

If he kept thinking about that, he was going to tear up again. It was time to start moving on. Somehow, he felt that would be a little easier after this chance encounter.

"Thank you." She held the fruitcake against her chest, staring at it as if it was something precious.

He put his arm around her as they headed for the door. He hadn't meant to do it, but it felt natural and she didn't object.

"You should know that a lot of people don't like fruitcake, either," he said. "But it could be a great paperweight or doorstop."

"It's heavy and solid. It would make a good projectile weapon." She grinned up at him.

"Well, don't go throwing it around on your spaceship. It'd probably go right through your windows."

She paused at the door and laughed. "Our viewports are

a bit stronger than that."

"Good. Because I don't want anything getting in the way of our second date."

"Date?" She cocked her head to the side.

"It's a custom among our people. We tend to pair off when we like each other to spend time and…"

She leaned in a bit closer. "Enjoy proximity?"

His mouth went dry. "Sometimes."

He cleared his throat, not knowing what to do. She had to leave, she had his number. If anything was going to happen between them, it was up to her now.

Well, maybe not entirely.

"There is one more Earth holiday tradition I could introduce you to," he said. "If you're interested."

"What's that?"

He pointed above the door, to the mistletoe hanging over their heads. "Mistletoe. When you're standing beneath it with someone you like, it's customary to…kiss them."

"Oh." She smiled. "That sounds pleasant."

"Wow." He couldn't hide his surprise. But before either of them could think themselves out of it, he pressed his lips against hers.

She leaned into him, her lips moving softly in response to his, almost tentatively. When he pulled back, her eyes were wide with wonder.

Never having tasted coffee he could believe. Never

hearing of Christmas... Okay, that was harder. But this being her first kiss... That was impossible. Right?

She blinked a few times, then looked away and laughed.

"I like this tradition," she said.

"Me, too."

As much as he wanted to hold on to the moment, he couldn't think of another reason to keep her. He opened the door and walked into the night, feeling a warmth in his chest that the chill air couldn't touch.

"I expected you back before now."

Ari's booming voice rumbled through the small shuttle as Vay strapped herself into the seat next to him at the pilot's console.

"My expedition was more fruitful than anticipated." She held up the gift Henry had given her and beamed at her pun. Vay would have to tell Evelyn about it when she returned from celebrating with her family.

Ari arched an eyebrow at the treasure in Vay's hands. "What is that?"

"Fruitcake."

"It looks like a nutrient brick."

Vay nodded. "That's what drew my attention. Its form and shape are like the food we're used to from the *Arbiter*.

But look at all the colors within it. Like the lights these Earthlings have used to decorate their town. We should share it with the others when we arrive at Homeworld Security headquarters."

"If you wish."

"I hear it's an acquired taste, though."

"You hear? From who?"

"I met a helpful Earthling."

"Most of them seem to be," Ari said. "It's an extraordinary planet on many levels."

He engaged the cloak that would obscure the vessel from the eyes of any curious Earthlings. Like Henry.

Ari paused in his launch preparations. "With you being our cultural programmer, I can justify stopping here to let you explore this town. But it was still unscheduled and we'll have to answer for it."

"I know," Vay said.

Ari was silent for a moment, then said, "Did you find what you were looking for?"

The lights had drawn her to the small town as they flew overhead. There was something almost magical about them. She'd had no idea what she was looking for when she asked Ari to make his stop. But she was absolutely sure she'd found it.

"Yes." Vay hadn't stopped smiling since she'd left Henry. Since he'd kissed her.

Ari smiled as well. "I'm glad. Then let's go."

Vay looked at the gift in her lap, then out the viewport. Her reflection beamed back at her in the transparent material, the bright, colorful lights illuminating the town below shining through.

Chapter One

A few weeks later…

"This is crazy." Vay repeated the statement as she walked toward the office of Earth's new planetary liaison, K-58-b7. Or, more simply, Kira.

Kira's bondmate, Brendan, stepped into the hallway. Vay quickly plastered a smile on her face. Hopefully, he hadn't heard her talking to herself.

"Hey, Vay." He used the same rhyming greeting every time they interacted.

"Hey, Brendan. Is Kira in her office?"

"You're in luck. She just returned from the Himalayas." His ever-present smile widened. "I still can't believe you can get from Asia to Montana in half an hour."

"Coalition shuttles are a good bit faster than anything you've developed on Earth," Vay said.

He chuckled. "Maybe a little."

She grinned, happy he was playing along with her understatement. "Is she alone?"

"Yeah. She dropped off Ari and Rin to look for the Centaurans. We may finally have a lead on where their base is located."

"Centaurans don't have bases. They're nomadic, even on their own homeworld."

"No wonder we're having trouble finding them. Kira's lucky Adam left you behind to help out with the search."

"Thanks, but I don't think he was actually planning for me to help hunt down the rogue sentients invading Earth. Having a cultural programmer around was probably more about setting up Earth's First Contact committee."

Brendan arched an eyebrow at her.

"Oh, right," she said. "I mean, 'Department of Homeworld Security'."

He stepped around her, walking backward up the hall so that he could maintain eye contact. "See, that's what I like about you, Vay. You respect our culture."

"That's what I'm here for." Vay turned as well and took a few steps backward, trying to mirror his motions, but bumped into a table. She twisted quickly and managed to catch a vase that had started to tip toward the floor.

Brendan chuckled. "See you at dinner."

"Yeah." Vay cautiously stepped away from the table as he disappeared down the stairs at the end of the hall. "Maybe."

Hopefully not.

Her stomach was churning. What was she doing? She wasn't a soldier like the others. Okay, technically, they were all soldiers in the great fleet of the Coalition of

Planets, but she was a scientist. A cultural programmer—one of the lowest ranking, most often denigrated positions in their entire society.

On a professional level, she found her fellow sentients' dismissal of her function fascinating. On a personal level, it "sucked ass", as Brendan would say.

The populations of new planets adapted to the Coalition's ways when they joined. It was mandatory. The only exceptions were the sentients who were physically incapable of imitating the dominant culture. And, if she was honest with herself, nobody in power cared about them.

The only Sadirians who cared about other cultures were the cultural programmers. And their job was supposed to be making life easier for the High Council and others in positions of power, not help the people being ruled.

"Why is this Antarean clicking at me? Is it an insult?"

"No, sir, that's just the noise their mandibles make when they're trying to form sounds in our language."

She was a facilitator, not a hunter. But Kira had limited resources, which presented Vay with an opportunity that she couldn't let pass by. She walked down the hallway with a more determined stride—being careful not to bump into any more furniture.

The door to Kira's office was open. Vay's heartbeat sped up. She had hoped she would have a few moments to build up her nerve to make her request, but Kira had probably heard her approach a mile away.

It was just an assignment—one that Vay desperately wanted. There was no harm in asking. Right?

"Are you just going to lurk in the hallway all day?"

Vay jumped at the low, strong voice echoing down the hall. There was no more time to second-guess herself. She quickly entered the office, hoping to appear confident instead of unprepared.

"Hi," Vay said. "I would ask how you heard me, but you did spend all that time running 'listening' stations." She made air-quotes around the word, the way Brendan had taught her.

Kira quirked up an eyebrow at the joke. And was that a hint of a smile?

Her dark hair was pulled back in a disheveled ponytail and there was a faint, yet distinct flush to her tanned skin. But then, Brendan had just been visiting, and Vay doubted he would have left without a kiss.

A strong pulse of excitement shot through her system at her own memory—a single kiss shared with a special Earthling on Christmas Eve that had changed Vay's world forever.

Suddenly fortified, she said, "I wanted to talk to you about the signal we detected today."

"What about it?"

"It's really close. Minutes away by shuttle. It's weak and didn't last more than a few seconds, but I think we should still investigate it."

"Yes, and if I had anyone to send, I'd have already—"

"Send me."

Kira's eyebrows shot up on her forehead. "You?"

"I can handle it. Like I said, it's only minutes away. It's probably nothing. A small-time operation or maybe just a signal that escaped from a sentient passing through that area."

"What if it's the Scorpiian bounty hunter that we know is operating on Earth? We still haven't tracked it down."

"I can send a distress call."

"You wouldn't get a chance. You'd never see it coming." The determined gleam that seemed to live in Kira's eyes was back. Vay felt her opportunity slipping away.

"It's probably nothing," Vay said.

"But it *could* be something."

Desperate, she reached for any way she could reassure Kira enough to send Vay to investigate. "A Scorpiian wouldn't have made the mistake of letting a signal be detected."

"No one is perfect. And even if the signal is from another rogue sentient, the Scorpiian might have picked up on it and be headed there to hunt whatever bounty is on the trespasser."

"Which makes it all the more important that we act quickly. We can track it down and—"

"There are too many unknowns." Kira shook her head. "Of all the assignments I've given out so far, this is the most dangerous. It makes more sense to wait and send Ari."

"I've received the same training, even if my skill set was weighted toward more diplomatic resolutions. Maybe that will work in my favor."

"Scorpiians aren't known for their love of diplomacy. They're more known for their ability to conceal themselves, get close to their targets, and kill them."

"I'm aware of that, sir. I also know that Scorpiians blend in to reach their targets, stalking and studying them so they can fool even the closest of friends. They don't just murder anyone who gets in their way—it would bring too much attention to them. And they wouldn't make the mistake of letting a signal like this slip through, no matter how faint it is. Like you said in this morning's meeting, it's likely just a false alarm. Why wait and send Ari to confirm that, when you can send me now?"

"What if it *is* the Scorpiian and it isn't following their standard cultural protocols? What if it's not a false alarm?"

"Then I'll gather intel—from my ship, flying cloaked and at night—and let you know what's going on. I can run passive scans during the day while my ship is safely hidden in the forest of the region. And if it is a Scorpiian, I'll turn around and come back here immediately. It'll never see me leaving."

Kira snorted. "You've been spending too much time with Brendan. His sense of humor is rubbing off on you." She fixed her dark eyes on Vay, all sense of amusement vanishing. "Why is this so important to you? Really?"

"I can't say, sir. But it is important to me. I've studied Earth customs enough to walk among them if necessary. I can be there and back in a couple of days."

"Vay, if this is about how many of us have pair-bonded with humans—"

She laughed. "I can honestly say that I'm not asking for this assignment in the hopes that I'll run into an Earthling and feel some sort of magical connection that I'm compelled to act on, falling hopelessly in love."

It was true. Because that had already happened. With a tall, somewhat gangly, brown-haired, brown-eyed Earthling.

Henry had the greatest smile. He'd made Vay laugh, even when she could tell that he'd been dealing with something that weighed on him. And he'd shared something of himself with her—the ways of his people, and his own kin. He'd made her feel part of something beautiful and special.

She hadn't had a chance to ask him what was bothering him at the time. Ari had been waiting for her in a shuttle nearby. They weren't supposed to make the stop, but she'd been drawn to the festive lights decorating the small town and wanted to understand what was happening.

Luckily, Kira had been forgiving of the little side-trip, especially when Vay spun it as a cultural observation submission. And it seemed luck was helping Vay out again. Henry lived very close to the signal's origin.

He'd given her his phone number. She could use that to triangulate his position. Maybe she could see him again, even just one more time. But only if she received the assignment.

Vay did her best not to fidget under Kira's intense stare. After a few more moments, Kira shook her head.

"Go. Report in every hour when you're not in your rest cycle."

Vay was stunned. Was she really being allowed to go?

"Standard procedure is every three hours."

Kira raised an eyebrow at her.

"But I'll report in every hour," Vay said. "Yes, sir. Thank you, sir."

She turned and practically ran from the room before Kira could change her mind.

Chapter Two

"This was a bad idea."

Henry stared at the ceiling of his parents' cabin, his gaze absently following the grain of the wooden beams. They had built most of the place with their own hands, using repurposed or other environmentally friendly materials. The cabin was filled with memories.

He couldn't sell it. He couldn't leave, either. Imagining it sitting empty in the forest was too...lonely.

"And I know something about that." He sighed and rolled onto his side. "Hence the talking to myself. Because there's no one else to talk to."

Maybe he could leave the cabin alone for a little while. Just until he'd had more time to grieve properly—around other people.

He wished he'd thought about the effects of being isolated while dealing with this before quitting his job. He hadn't been thinking clearly at the time.

All he'd thought was that his inheritance would be enough for him to live on for years and he could always find another high school that needed a biology teacher. And he'd had something in mind to keep him busy.

"Get going, Henry." He spoke in his best imitation of his dad, imagining his advice. Moving into their cabin so Henry could look for evidence of a Sasquatch probably wouldn't be among it.

He deepened his voice again. "If you're going to look for Bigfoot, go look for Bigfoot. Get off the damned couch."

Henry laughed, almost feeling like his dad was with him again. He sat up and stretched.

"Cryptozoology is tangentially related to biology," Henry said. "So it's kind of like work."

Dad wouldn't necessarily have agreed, but he would have been amused and supportive. He'd have joined Henry on his walks through the woods, looking for evidence of cryptids—lifeforms that may or may not exist outside of legend. Henry smiled as he stood and walked across the room to grab his coat from the peg where it hung by the door, glad that he'd remembered it this time.

"Get going, Henry," he said, in dad's voice. "Something great is just on the other side of that door."

Cold swept over him as he opened the door. Something great *was* on the other side. Well, som*eone* great.

"Vay?"

Her blue eyes were wide as she stared at him, one hand poised as if she'd been about to knock when he opened the door. Her short blonde hair stuck out from underneath the same silly Christmas hat that she'd been wearing the night they met—Christmas Eve. And she had on the ridiculous, eye-jarring moose sweater in half a dozen clashing bright colors.

All of that came to him from his peripheral vision, because he couldn't look away from her face. Those beautiful eyes and perfect features. Pert nose, gently curved lips.

Soft lips... He knew from their experience under the mistletoe. His skin was suddenly tingling, and not from the cold.

"Hi." A wisp of a smile pulled at the corners of her mouth.

"Hi. Hi," he repeated, shock giving way to enthusiasm.

Vay was here. Here!

Before he could think better of it, he stepped forward and picked her up in a huge hug, swinging her around in a circle and laughing. He couldn't believe how much he had missed her. She wrapped her arms tightly around his neck, her laughter merging with his and ringing through the trees.

As he set her down, she smiled at him. It warmed him better than any coat would. He loved her smile— especially how her front teeth stuck out just a tiny bit more than the others. It was the one imperfection to her features that made her beauty that much more real.

"I'm not imagining you, am I?" he said.

"No. Unless I'm imagining you, too."

He shook his head. "Not that I'm aware of. What are you doing here?"

"Working up the nerve to knock on your door?"

They both laughed again.

"I happened to be in the neighborhood, and you'd extended that kind invitation..." she said.

"Of course! Come in."

He stepped back into the cabin, drawing her in after him. He closed the door, then helped her take off her coat. There was a rug inside to deal with the snow crusting her boots, some of which had already fallen onto his coat that was lying on the floor. He didn't even remember dropping it. He picked it up and hung it on a hook next to Vay's.

For a moment, he was stunned, looking at their coats next to each other on the hooks. He wanted to keep seeing them that way with a need that made it hard for him to catch his breath—and also was completely ridiculous. How could he have such strong feelings about her after spending less than an hour in her company?

He knew he'd been smitten with her the night they met. It had felt like more than infatuation, though. It still did.

Thinking about her gave him the happiest moments he'd experienced in months, even when he'd thought they would never see each other again. She'd left him with the distinct impression that her life was too busy to give her room for socializing. But now she was standing next to him and it felt...right.

Her gaze drifted from the kitchen area to the rustic furniture, fireplace, and loft above. Her lips were slightly parted and her eyes were wide. He hoped that meant she liked it.

The stones surrounding the fireplace were still warm from last night's fire and the potbelly stove near the kitchen was full of chunks of burning wood. The cabin was pretty cozy. Or it would be with a few quilts. And thermal underwear.

Henry and his parents had worked hard to make the space inviting and beautiful. It was just as gorgeous from the outside, with two-story timber walls and a wood-shingle roof covered in snow. He'd strung solar-powered Christmas lights all around it after he and Vay had met. Their battery charged up all day so they could shine through most of the night when the light sensors kicked them on. The place was like a postcard, inside and out.

"You live here?" she said.

"I do."

"It's lovely."

He laughed, remembering the running gag from their first conversation. "Not bad for a primitive planet."

"What?" She looked genuinely shocked—and a little scared, which was strange.

"Sorry, I was just doing a call-back to Christmas Eve. Remember, I kept making jokes about you being from another planet because you'd never heard of Christmas?"

Or birthdays. Or tasted coffee.

He still hadn't figured out how she was so sheltered, but he had a few ideas. The most probable theory was that she'd been raised in some sort of cultist compound. His favorite idea was that she actually *was* an alien. He felt his smile broaden at the thought, but managed not to tell her about it.

"Right. The joke." She let out a nervous laugh.

He tried to shift the conversation toward something that would help put her at ease, but barreled right into probably the least safe topic.

"How long are you in town for?"

Please say, 'forever', he chanted in his mind.

"A few days."

"Oh." He tried to hide his disappointment. He wasn't sure how successful he was.

Vay took his hand in hers. "But I'd like to spend them with you. If that's okay."

"Okay? That's great."

He was relieved when her smile became more relaxed.

"I can make us hot cocoa," he said. "I promise you'll like it much more than coffee."

She made a face and laughed. "That wouldn't be hard. I tried to develop a taste for coffee, like you said people do, but still haven't managed."

"If you hate it so much, why bother?"

"It reminded me of you."

She must have seen how stunned he was at her admission, because she said, "What?"

"It's nothing. I'm just glad to know you thought of me since Christmas."

"You made quite an impression," she said.

"A good one, I hope."

"You could say that."

She was here, after all. How had she even found his cabin? Maybe she asked around town. He didn't want to look too closely at this...miracle.

"My work takes place mostly at night," she said. "But I should have a few hours in the afternoons and evenings."

"That's fine. You can take naps here." He gestured to the couch and the loft upstairs. Warmth flooded his body at the thought of her in his bed—even alone.

Or not...

"That's sweet, but my superiors probably wouldn't approve of that. I need to check in with them frequently."

"Right. That makes sense." Sort of. His theory about her being in a cult was gaining traction. "Have you eaten? I could make us something."

"I'm not hungry, but thanks." She angled her head toward the couch and shrugged one shoulder. "Could we sit and talk?"

"Sure."

No matter what she needed or why she was here, he was grateful to be with her again. And if this was all they could have—just a few days—he'd gladly take any and every moment she could share with him.

Chapter Three

Vay let out a huge yawn as she flew in yet another widening circle over the forest. She'd only managed to get a couple of hours in her regen bed and she couldn't have cared less. Her cheeks were tired from laughing, making her that much more aware of the smile that seemed to be permanently installed on her face.

She'd spent the day with Henry. Almost the entire day. Aside from dodging a few uncomfortable questions about how she had found him, she had even managed to be mostly open and honest with him.

She'd had to be careful that he didn't figure out the truth about her. The last thing she wanted was for him to receive a mind-wipe.

Somehow, knowing that he was thinking about her and had fond memories of their time together on Christmas Eve made her feel a warmth deep in her body unlike anything she'd ever experienced. It was like happiness, only more intense. And it was systemic.

She wriggled in her chair a bit, as thinking about him made her belly fill with tingling energy. Energy that spread lower, making her ache in a way she hadn't been able to work up the nerve to explore. Yet.

It was new. Everything with him was new. And she wanted to experience whatever she could in the time they had.

If only there were more of it.

A light flickered to life on her command console. Not from the scans she was running, searching for that errant signal, but from the communications array. She'd forgotten to check in.

"Crap."

Kira was going to be unhappy. She might even pull Vay back to the mansion where the First Contact committee was headquartered.

There was no way she would leave without saying goodbye to Henry. But she wasn't ready to do that yet.

She would just have to talk Kira into letting Vay stay. She tapped on the control to open the connection, feeling her smile fade to more normal levels.

Instead of her commanding officer's angular features filling the com-screen, she saw a man with a strong chin and narrow eyes. His complete lack of hair was helpful in jarring her out of her surprise.

"Ari? I thought you were in the Himalayas."

"I am. And I see where you've been assigned."

Double-crap.

Ari had been piloting the shuttle when Vay insisted on making the stop in the nearby town. He'd risked getting a reprimand by indulging her curiosity.

"I forgot to check in," she said. "I need to send my 'all's well' code."

"I sent it for you. I know that Kira is holding everyone to extremely high standards in following protocols."

He was covering for her. Again.

"Kira's not that bad. She's new to being planetary liaison, and doesn't want to do anything that will endanger us making our case to the High Council on behalf of Earth."

General Serath—Adam—and his Earthling bondmate Evelyn were en route to Sadr-4 to try to convince the leaders of the Coalition to establish a First Contact committee on Earth. It was much earlier than was standard procedure, but the circumstances were highly unusual.

For one thing, the previous planetary liaison was in General Serath's brig awaiting trial. And for another, the growing number of Earthlings who had learned of the alien operations on Earth had already taken matters into their own hands, forming the Department of Homeworld Security.

Two of the Earthlings on Earth's ad-hoc First Contact committee had joined Serath to both observe and help make their case—Brendan's sister, Paige, and his government liaison, Eric.

Paige was an environmental scientist, and planned to offer her skills and knowledge of Earth's incredible resources to help restore the ecosystems of planets that couldn't support life without domes anymore.

Eric was going along to negotiate on Earth's behalf and offer a less overt boon to the Coalition. He and Sorca were pair-bonded, as baffling as that still was to Vay. And Sorca planned to leave the fleet to stay on Earth with Eric if the Department of Homeworld Security wasn't officially recognized.

Given her cultural assessment of the High Council, Vay doubted it would be enough to have Earth's First Contact committee approved. All the more reason to enjoy her time with Henry while she could. If she had any more.

"You can relax. This transmission has been encrypted so that no one can listen in," Ari said.

"How did you manage that?"

"Brendan. His understanding of our communications technology is impressive."

If only Henry had a skill like that to offer. Maybe he could join Earth's First Contact committee as well. He wouldn't need a mind-wipe then. They could be together, like the others and their bondmates.

"Vay, we can't do anything that might hurt the chances of Earth's First Contact committee being recognized."

Ari's booming voice was stern. Almost like he was giving her a warning. He couldn't know about Henry, could he?

"I want Earth to be safe," she said. "I won't jeopardize

that."

"Good." He let out a long sigh. "The last time we were in this area and we made that stop—"

Triple-crap. He knew something.

"Ari, don't."

Brendan might have helped Ari encode their communication, but she still wasn't comfortable with them coming out and talking about Henry openly. There was no such thing as a completely secure system.

"Listen to me," Ari said. "You came back changed. You'd found that...celebratory fruitcake. Maybe no one else noticed, but you and I have been stationed together since we were first assigned to the fleet. I know how much of an impression that fruitcake made on you. Earth fruitcake is appealing. I get that. The pretty colors, the flavors—"

"I didn't eat it," she said.

"What?"

"I couldn't bring myself to. It's too pretty. I put it in a stasis pod."

That she kept under her pillow back in her room. Ari didn't need to know that.

She knew she'd derailed his metaphor. She wanted him to stop talking about it—to stop talking about Henry. But Ari was stubborn.

He ran a hand over his face. When he looked at her again, his eyes were full of sympathy. Maybe even pity.

"A stasis pod is a good place for it," he said. "You can think about it and remember whatever fun you had finding that fruitcake. But you can't take it back to the *Arbiter* with you. You can't hold on to that fruitcake forever. Eventually, you're going to have to let it go. The sooner you do, maybe the less it will hurt."

"I appreciate you looking out for me. I really do. But this is my decision. If I want to experience more fruitcake, that's my choice."

He shook his head and mumbled, "What is it about this planet?"

"Ari?"

"Yeah?"

"Thank you."

He let out a little snort and smirked. "Just looking out for my team. Watch your back, okay? Earth isn't all fun and fruitcakes. And with a Scorpiian running planetside, we all need to be careful."

"I will be." She thought of an Earth expression that matched very well with Ari's mission tracking down the Centaurans he was after. "Good hunting."

He snorted again, his smile widening. "Safe journeys."

The transmission ended. Vay felt a lump form in her throat.

Whatever else was happening on and with Earth, this assignment was bringing the people she was stationed with closer together. It was making what they did more meaningful somehow. She hoped that would last when they all were inevitably reassigned.

Chapter Four

"Brachiation. That would explain it." Henry looked up at the bare trees surrounding him. "If they get around by swinging through the trees, they wouldn't leave much evidence behind."

The fog from his breath puffed around his face in a billowing cloud. Once again, he'd forgotten his scarf. And hat. And gloves. At least he wasn't planning to stay out long.

"Except they're famous for leaving footprints." He returned his gaze to the snow-covered ground. "Big footprints—hence the name. But even that evidence isn't too common, so maybe... Maybe I should stop talking to myself."

And save his voice for Vay. She'd be at the cabin in a few hours. He hoped whatever work she'd done the night before had gone well and that she was getting some rest. He couldn't wait to see her again.

They had talked all day yesterday. All day, and he never once became bored or tired. He realized the newness of their relationship was contributing to how well things seemed to be going. They'd also spent a lot of time talking about his favorite topics, like scifi movies and books—which seemed to absolutely fascinate her. But even the lulls in the conversations had been companionable.

He loved spending time with her. He'd never clicked with anyone like he did with Vay. It was amazing.

A stick cracked loudly ahead of him, pulling him out of his thoughts and back into his surroundings. The hairs on his arms stood on end. He should have been paying more attention.

Aside from the recent cold snap and thick snow, the winter had been relatively mild. The black bears in the region had been known to leave their dens throughout the winter when the oak trees had a good crop of acorns. Like the trees he was walking through at that moment.

"Please don't be a bear."

He looked up into the dark eyes of a black bear.

"When I thought climate change was a threat to my existence, this is not what I pictured."

The bear let out a low growl.

"Easy, fella." Henry tried to remember what to do. His thoughts were scattered. "When a bear attacks, I'm supposed to try to look big, right? And make a lot of noise?"

The bear charged him.

"Oh, crap."

Henry started waving his arms above his head and jumping up and down. He yelled as loud as he could, making gibberish sounds that grew more desperate by the second.

The bear suddenly skidded to a halt only a few feet away. It turned around, and with a startled roar, it ran away.

Henry stared after it, wondering what had just happened. Then he started to laugh.

"I can't believe that worked."

His skin still felt electrified from the adrenaline. He let his head drop back, eyes closed and face pointed toward the sky. Relief washed over him as he took deep, steadying breaths—until he felt warm breath flow over his face in return.

"I'm going to open my eyes now," he said. "And I am not going to see a bear about to drop on my face."

He slowly turned around as he opened his eyes, looking up at whatever was in the tree above him. Only it wasn't in the tree. It was standing, hovering over him.

Henry stumbled backward, tripped over his own feet, and landed hard on his ass. His brain struggled to process what he was seeing.

"Oh my God."

He was staring at a seven-and-a-half foot tall Sasquatch. A Sasquatch!

Its face had a flat nose and broad mouth surrounded by bluish-tinged, wrinkled skin. Most of its head and all of its body was covered in a thick coat of white fur. Its eyes were bright blue, with horizontal pupils that almost bisected its irises.

"Gorilla," he muttered to himself. "It's like a giant, albino gorilla. Except for the eyes... Blue, not pink."

The Sasquatch planted two of its arms on its hips...and crossed the other pair over its chest.

Four arms. Four. Arms.

Henry's throat was so tight, it hurt to swallow. The creature leaned forward and exhaled another huge breath from its nostrils, blowing Henry's hair away from his face.

"An albino gorilla?" Its deep voice sounded remarkably...huffy. "That is offensive."

Henry let out a high-pitched laugh. "It can talk. Of course it can talk. Because this is a delusion. I've obviously gone insane."

"Excuse me, but I'm not an 'it'. I'm male."

The Sasquatch stood up and fluffed the fur around its cheeks. At least, it *looked* like fur. Until it sharpened into stiff quills that quivered like a defensive porcupine's.

"I'm sorry," Henry said. "This is kind of new to me. I've never met a Sasquatch before."

"A what?"

"A Sasquatch. You know—Bigfoot? Yeti? Gigantopithecus?" He always looked to the fossil record first to explain cryptids.

It—he—the Bigfoot rolled his eyes. It extended one of its arms to the ground to balance as it lifted a foot, and pointed at it with yet another arm. "Do my feet look big to you?"

"Uh, proportionally? I guess not. But I don't know what else to call you."

"How about 'Craig'?"

"Why would I call you that?"

"Because it's my chosen Earth name."

"Earth name..."

Henry's heartbeat sped up. He'd always dismissed the possibility of cryptids being of extra-terrestrial origin. But seeing 'Craig' in the flesh, it made a hell of a lot more sense than this lifeform evolving from something native to Earth.

"You're an alien," Henry said.

"I'm a Lyrian. Educate yourself." Craig huffed out another big breath through his nostrils. "But I suppose that would be futile. If you did learn anything about us, the Sadirians would swoop in and erase your memories. You can't throw a tnergog without them trying to give somebody a mind-wipe."

The Sasquatch... Lyrian... *Craig* made an offhanded gesture with one of his arms.

Henry didn't know how to respond to Craig's statement. He was having trouble forming coherent thoughts. To make things worse, his nose started to tingle a moment before he let out a huge sneeze. He managed to turn his head to the side at the last instant.

Craig pounded two of his hands into the ground on either side of Henry's legs and let out an ear-splitting roar that sounded like a cross between an angry bear and a constipated elephant. Henry caught a glimpse of teeth as he fell backward—so many teeth—like the inside of a Great White's mouth.

"Please don't eat me," he yelled. "It was just a sneeze."

"What is 'sneeeeeze'?" Craig drew out the word.

"It's an involuntary reaction to being exposed to allergens, bright light, or cold." Henry recited the definition like he was back in front of his class. "It's just how the human body clears out its sinus passages and nostrils."

Craig glared at Henry for what felt like a long time. He wasn't sure if he should be trying to make eye contact or avoid it. The last thing he wanted to do was make Craig feel challenged.

After a few more moments, Craig sat back on the ground. "*Sneeze* is weird."

"Yeah." Henry stifled another near-hysterical laugh. He didn't know what might set Craig off.

"This whole situation is kind of weird to me, too," Henry continued. "But I promise, I don't want to hurt you."

Craig's lips twitched up on one side. A smirk? Henry wondered if it meant the same thing to a Lyrian.

"Not that I could if I tried," Henry said. "But I wouldn't

try. I'm not that kind of person."

"And what kind of person are you?"

Henry sat up, very slowly. "I'm a biology teacher. I study the lifeforms on my planet and teach children about them."

"A noble task." Craig's eyebrows rose. He looked sincerely impressed.

Henry couldn't keep himself from letting out a little snort of derision. "I wish all the other Earthlings felt that way." When Craig cocked his head to the side, Henry added, "Many of the people where I'm from don't actually value teachers much."

"That's foolish," Craig said.

"Tell me about it. I'm Henry, by the way. That's my name."

"Henry."

They sat on the ground, Craig staring intently at Henry, while Henry did his best to only make occasional eye contact. The ground was freezing, and the cold started to get to him. He pulled his coat around himself more tightly.

"You lack fur," Craig said.

"Yeah. For the most part." Henry laughed, then ruffled his hair. "I have this, at least."

"That is insufficient."

"Well, I forgot my hat and scarf at home. And my gloves." He dropped his hands onto his lap just as his stomach let out a loud gurgle.

Craig was on him again in an instant, teeth bared as he knocked Henry backward onto the ground.

"It was just my stomach growling," Henry yelled.

Craig kept hovering over Henry, but seemed to relax.

"Is it angry?" Craig asked.

"What? No." Henry let out a little laugh, more relief than amusement. "It means I'm hungry. I sort of forgot to eat breakfast this morning, too."

Craig exhaled sharply. "Earthling, where are your parents?"

Even if Craig wasn't an alien, he couldn't have known how his question would hit Henry right in the gut. He almost preferred when the Lyrian was getting in his face. Terror was easier to handle than the weight of his grief.

When he'd been talking to Vay, it was the first time that Henry had felt anywhere close to normal in as long as he could remember. He'd been careful to avoid the topic of his parents—which was probably part of why he hadn't learned much about her own upbringing.

"They died a couple of months ago," Henry said. "Car accident."

Craig's eyebrows rose again, his jaw going slack so that his mouth hung open. "You're an orphan?"

"I guess so, technically. But I'm self-sufficient."

"You ventured into a cold environment without proper coverings and neglected to feed yourself."

Henry shook his head and laughed. "Well, when you

put it like that…" He wished Craig would give him a little more space "I'm dealing with it. I'm twenty-six, I can—"

"Twenty-six? As in twenty-six Earth solar cycles?"

"Yes." Henry didn't like the way Craig was looking at him. Was that pity? Concern? "Which means I'm an adult. I can take care of myself."

"Obviously not." Craig puffed out another breath, looming even closer. He slid two of his arms under Henry's back and picked him up with no apparent effort.

"What are you doing?"

"Taking you someplace warm where there is food."

Craig wrapped even more of his arms across Henry's body, holding him close to his chest. His fur was unbelievably soft and warm. It was like being carried by a giant kitten. A many-armed, bizarrely protective kitten.

"This isn't necessary," Henry said.

"Of course it isn't."

It might have been Henry's imagination, but he thought there was a bit of a purring noise coming from Craig's chest as he spoke. The condescension came through loud and clear, even if it was intended kindly.

"I'm glad you see it that way." He waited for Craig to put him down. Instead, the Lyrian kept walking, his stride carrying them quickly through the forest. "Um, Craig?"

"Yes, Henry?"

"You can put me down now. Like I said, I can take care of myself."

Craig chuckled. "Your mental acuity seems to be suffering. Perhaps you need sleep as well."

"I don't need sleep."

If Henry fell asleep—which was never going to happen while he was in the care of an alien—he might miss his time with Vay later. The fact that his mind immediately went to her when he was being carried through the forest by an alien Sasquatch told him how far gone his heart already was.

"I am a full-grown adult," Henry said.

"Nestlings are so cute at this stage. They've just grown their first pair of arms and think they can take on the world."

"I don't want to take on the— Wait, did you say *first* pair of arms?"

Craig ignored the statement.

"I've been watching you roam around the forest for a while now," he said. "What were you looking for?"

Henry let out a defeated sigh. "You."

"Well, then. Congratulations."

"Thanks."

Chapter Five

After another reduced cycle in the regen bed, Vay knew she should be feeling tired. Instead, she was invigorated. She couldn't wait to peel off her uniform and put on her Earth clothes.

She'd only brought along the one outfit, though. If she had packed more, it might have raised suspicions. Kira was being a bit overprotective and had checked several times to make sure Vay had everything she needed for the assignment. And Vay wasn't supposed to leave the ship unless absolutely necessary.

She was also supposed to be spending her "down time" in the afternoons and evenings going over the data she was collecting both on her nightly patrols and during the stationary scans her ship conducted each day. Technically, she did review everything as soon as she ended her rest cycle. It just didn't take that long. There hadn't been any more anomalous readings.

She grabbed a nutrient brick and sat at the console, staring at the scrolling information. Her stomach rebelled at the once-familiar substance.

Ari's warning came back to her with jarring force. She

shouldn't get attached to anything on Earth. They'd have to go back to Sadr-4 eventually—and the space stations, ships, and dome-worlds. Her future was filled with nutrient bricks.

No more pancakes. No more fuzzy sweaters. No more Christmas lights or fresh air.

No more Henry.

Her eyes blurred. She couldn't even wipe them clear on her uniform. The material was hydrophobic, and would just sort of smear her tears around. Instead, she blinked rapidly until her vision improved.

Too many of the Sadirian soldiers who had visited Earth were pair-bonding with Earthlings. Even if Henry eventually fell in love with Vay, there was no way to know if she'd be permitted to stay.

The High Council found it hard to believe that anyone would give up access to their technology to remain on a relatively primitive world, and required an incredible amount of investigation, interviews, and testing to allow it.

If they granted her request, it would mean her Coalition citizenship would be revoked and Vay would be banished to Earth forever. That would be a dream come true. But she had to be honest with herself. It was very unlikely to happen.

It would be much easier if Henry decided to come with her to live aboard the *Arbiter*—or wherever else she was stationed. The Coalition could find something for him to do, and they were much more understanding of someone from one of those "primitive planets" wanting to improve their circumstances by bonding with a Coalition citizen.

Less bureaucracy to navigate, but a much bigger sacrifice. She wouldn't let Henry give up Earth to be with her—even if his feelings for her ever became strong enough for him to make the offer.

She pounded on a disposal port to open it, then dropped in the barely-eaten remains of her nutrient brick. At least it wouldn't be wasted. The tiny shuttle she was using would sterilize and recycle it into her next meal.

Maybe Henry would offer to cook for her again.

She should just be happy with the time he was giving her. And she was actually learning so much about Earth's cultures from talking to him through the game they'd accidentally begun. He thought she was playing along when he spoke to her as if she was from another planet. If only he knew the truth.

She was sure he wouldn't freak out if she told him. He would accept her for what she was.

She hoped.

Maybe she could convince Kira to request that Vay be permanently reassigned to Earth. Most of the sentient species that the Coalition had discovered were already integrated into their culture. They didn't need many cultural programmers anymore, which she was actually glad for.

The High Council usually waited for a planet to have a single, homogenous culture before approaching them about joining the Coalition. They said it made it easier for them to adapt, but Vay knew the truth. It wasn't about adaptation—it was about conquest. Her predecessors had assisted in the obliteration of countless cultures.

They'd provided the High Council with reports and ideas on how best to get other sentients to adapt to the ways of the Sadirians, who held most of the power in the galaxy through their much more advanced technology. Surely some of those cultural programmers had hated what they were forced to do as much as Vay did.

Being assigned to the *Arbiter*, Vay was able to study the few sentients who couldn't—or wouldn't—conform. She provided information on how to help them adapt that was...not exactly helpful. She made sure her data was just good enough to keep her on the *Arbiter*, but didn't give the Coalition anything that could actually help them destroy those cultures.

She didn't see the harm in preserving other ways of life. Earth was a perfect example, with so many different sub-cultures within each culture even. If they could make that work and actually help each other, which many Earthlings did, surely the Coalition could as well.

The Antareans, with their intricate hive societies, could teach Sadirians about caring for their communities. Lyrians could teach them about familial bonds, which they formed with a speed and passion that was only matched by their formidable tempers.

Every sentient had worth. Why couldn't the High Council see—

A flashing light finally snapped Vay out of her thoughts. Moons, she knew she had a tendency to get caught up in her own head, but she'd blanked out on screens and screens of data. Luckily, she'd programmed the computer to double-check her work and notify her of anomalies. Like the one blinking on her screen.

"What is that?" She pulled up the data and looked at the screen more closely.

Another anomalous reading. It looked like residual energy left from another sort of scan—one she wasn't familiar with. She compared her earlier readings of the area, fine-tuning the shuttle's systems to look for that particular signature. They were faint, but she could see a definite pattern.

Something had conducted a scan in a broad circular area using a technology she wasn't familiar with—that *her ship* wasn't familiar with. And her shuttle was equipped with the most advanced Coalition tech available.

This was new. It was powerful. And Henry's cabin was within its field of scrutiny.

"Crap."

There was no time to change into her Earth clothes, and her shuttle was grounded. The area was somewhat remote, but popular with campers and hikers. She couldn't risk her ship being detected. If she took off in the middle of the day—cloak or no—Kira would pull her back to headquarters immediately.

Vay wanted to grab a phase rifle to take along, but there were too many unknowns. If she dropped it or someone managed to take it from her, everyone would be pulled from the Earth assignment and Serath's chances of getting the First Contact committee recognized would be ruined.

Her wristband had a built in weapon as well as a shield. It would have to be enough.

She hit the control to close her helmet. The segments clicked rapidly into place, then fused. For a split second, the opaque metal left her in complete darkness, but then the internal screens flickered to life, giving her a view of her surroundings along with additional readouts and her uniform's functional levels.

Within moments, she was outside in the forest, running toward Henry's cabin. She would make a quick pass to confirm that everything seemed okay, taking care that he didn't see her in her uniform, then investigate more of the scan area she'd detected.

"Activate bio-sensor."

A grid appeared in her field of vision—tiny specks of light showing her where small animals were located outside. If anything bigger drew near, her uniform would warn her before she was close enough to be seen or heard.

"Everything's going to be fine," she said. "Henry is fine."

He had to be.

Chapter Six

"If you've been watching me all this time, how did I never notice you?" Henry couldn't believe he was adjusting to being carried by a giant fur-covered alien. "You're not exactly inconspicuous."

Craig chuckled. "Lyrians are masters of disguise. Our coats can change to match our environment, see?"

He seemed to disappear into thin air as Henry watched. He felt Craig's fur ripple where they touched, and could see a vague outline where he knew Craig was, but that was it. After a few seconds, Craig became opaque again.

"How did you do that?" Henry said.

"My spines are able to bend light. It's useful for eluding capture, but makes more sentients interested in catching us."

"I don't understand."

"We don't have to be in our skins for our spines to work. Our pelts can be made into the ultimate camouflage uniforms."

Henry was stunned. His stomach started to cramp up as he thought of the implications. "I can't even imagine someone being capable of doing that. Are you safe on

Earth?"

"I appreciate your concern." Craig glanced down at him and smiled, that small purring sound rumbling in his chest again. "We're as safe here as anywhere in the galaxy."

"Wait... We?"

"My mate, Barbara, is here as well."

"Craig and Barbara?" Henry laughed. "How do you have such ordinary names?"

"Our language isn't biologically compatible with your species."

"As in, our anatomy can't pronounce it?"

Craig snorted. "More like, if exposed to it for prolonged periods of time, your eardrums might rupture. Plus, it tends to carry, and would make us easier to detect. We selected Earth names to use for the duration of our mission."

"That's...great."

Henry had so many questions. About their physiology, where they were from, what life was like on their planet—and on others, if they knew about them. But there was one answer he needed before he satisfied his scientific curiosity.

"What is your mission on Earth?"

"Don't worry, we're here as collectors, not conquerors."

"I'd feel a lot better about that if you weren't carrying me to an undisclosed location."

Craig laughed, a loud, rumbling sound that made Henry

smile despite his worry.

"We're collecting seeds. Some we gather ourselves, and others we trade for."

"Trade with whom?" Henry tried to imagine what that exchange would look like. For some reason, he pictured Craig wearing a giant raincoat and Fedora, like in the movies.

"There are a few open-minded humans who have agreed to assist us in exchange for certain materials and equipment that assist them in their research."

Humans working with aliens for scientific research? Henry wanted in on that. Well, as long as Earth wouldn't suffer for it.

"Are you sure that's safe? I mean, what are those humans even using your stuff for?"

"We don't ask." Craig sniffed. "That would be rude."

Henry hesitated to ask his next question, but felt he had to. "And what are *you* using *our* stuff for?"

"Once we have enough seeds that can be modified to fit in with various ecosystems, we'll replicate them in our lab so we can distribute them to those in need."

"That doesn't sound so bad," Henry murmured.

"It won't negatively impact Earth in the slightest, and will greatly improve living conditions for several sentient species who have been victimized by the Sadirians." He sneered as he said the word.

"You mentioned them before. I take it you don't like

them very much."

"They are evil, Henry. All they care about is control. They come in offering technology that can improve life for everyone on a planet—at a price. They start small, making trades that seem completely reasonable. But once the sentients are addicted to their technology and think that's all they need to survive, the Sadirians strip the planet of resources. The population becomes completely dependent on them for survival."

Henry shivered. He wasn't sure if it was from the cold or the idea of such a cruel civilization.

"Don't worry, nestling," Craig said. "We're well hidden from the Sadirians who are on Earth."

"I'm not a nes— Wait, did you say 'on Earth'? As in, there are Sadirians on Earth right now?"

"Among others."

"Others..."

Henry was having trouble wrapping his mind around the concept of Earth being filled with different kinds of extraterrestrials. How many cryptids might actually be from other planets? How many were threats?

"The Sadirians aren't invading, are they?" he asked. "Or planning to offer Earth their technology?"

He had no illusions about Earth's ability to resist such an offer. Human greed was already damaging the planet. If the Sadirians were everything Craig said they were, they would only make things worse.

"Honestly, I'm not sure," he said. "But Barbara and I will protect you. Don't worry."

Before Henry could yet again explain that he didn't need to be protected and could take care of himself, the forest around them vanished. It just disappeared, replaced with smooth walls made of some sort of greenish metal. Lights blinked here and there, and he could hear the hum of machinery around him.

"What just happened?" Henry said.

Craig grinned. "Welcome to our home."

"Craig, sweetheart, the new samples are—" The new voice sounded much the same as Craig's. If anything, it was a little deeper. Barbara?

Craig pressed Henry closer, partially covering Henry's body with the spines of his chest.

"Before you get angry," Craig said, "let me explain."

"Explain... What is that you're carrying?" she said.

"You know that Earthling I've been watching?"

"Yes." She dragged out the word.

"He was attacked by a bear, so I—"

Barbara let out a sigh deep enough to ruffle Henry's hair. She must be standing right next to them. Henry tried to crane his neck to look at her, but Craig was holding him too close.

"So you ran to the rescue," she said. "Why in the name of the Solar Cross did you bring him back to our ship? You're risking everything."

"You risked the same when you decided to help that Earthling Carol and her son."

Henry could feel the low vibration of Craig's growling voice through his chest. He did not want to be in the middle of a fight between two space-Sasquatches. Wriggling out of Craig's four-armed embrace didn't seem feasible, though.

Barbara's voice held an answering growl. "That was different. She needed help creating medicine."

"Henry needs help, too," Craig said. "He's an orphan."

Henry blew the spine-fur out of his mouth so he could speak. "Pheh. Pheh. I am not. I mean, technically, I am, but I'm an adult."

"He's cold and he's hungry and he's all alone," Craig said.

Cold and hungry, yes. But not alone. Not since Vay had shown up on his doorstep. But then, Craig probably didn't know about her. He might not have followed Henry back as far as his cabin while "observing the human in the wild".

Craig leaned closer to Barbara and lowered his voice, as if he thought he could whisper quietly enough that Henry wouldn't hear him. "And he's only twenty-six Earth cycles old."

"Twenty-six?" There was a catch in Barbara's voice.

Here we go.

"Twenty-six is considered mature for my species,"

Henry insisted.

Barbara brushed Craig's fur away from Henry's face, giving him a chance to finally see her. She pretty much looked exactly like Craig, except the fur around her face was much shorter, revealing more of her ears. They were shaped sort of like bat wings. They even moved like wings as she studied him.

"Cool…"

Henry shook himself, gently pushing away from Craig's chest. Now was not the time to be studying Lyrian physiology.

When his feet were on the floor of what must be their spaceship, he could see an opening behind Craig that led to the forest. Henry had been in this area dozens of times recently and seen nothing out of place.

"Is your ship invisible?" Henry asked.

"Yes." Craig puffed up his chest and smiled. "Lyrians are at the forefront of cloaking technology. Not that anyone knows, thanks to Sadirians stealing all the credit."

Barbara's lips peeled back from her teeth and she hissed at Craig. A second row of teeth protruded from inside her mouth.

"Darling, let's be civil," Craig said. "You're scaring Henry."

"I'm fine." Henry did his best to hide his fear—and keep from losing control of any bodily functions—while Barbara calmed down.

Once her teeth were back in a more familiar configuration she exhaled sharply like Craig often did. She glared at Henry, making his palms sweat.

"He looks like a Tau Ceti," she said.

Craig smiled, as if that was a compliment. Henry tried to follow his lead.

"Thanks?"

The corner of Barbara's mouth quirked up. He hoped that was a good thing.

She turned back toward the archway where she'd come from. "I knew I should have agreed when you asked to breed more nestlings."

As soon as she was gone, Craig pulled Henry into a crushing hug while ruffling his hair.

So many arms…

"She likes you," Craig said.

"Really. How could you tell?"

Craig let Henry go and shrugged. "She didn't tear off any of your arms."

"Ha ha." Henry followed Craig deeper into the ship. "Wait, you were joking, right? Right?"

Chapter Seven

"Stop freaking out." Vay repeated the words over and over again, not that it was helping.

Henry wasn't at his cabin. But the energy signature she'd been tracking was.

It was so faint, if she hadn't known what to look for, she wouldn't have noticed it. But there were definite traces of energy all over his home. Her heart hadn't stopped pounding since she'd left.

She wasn't sure how or why, but she was certain it was the Scorpiian. For a single, crazy moment, she wondered if maybe it and Henry were one and the same. Disguising itself as a human would be exactly the kind of thing it would do to blend in and get close to its target. But she just couldn't believe that was true.

Henry was kind and warm. He was loving and gentle.

Scorpiians were cold assassins. She would have picked up on that while they talked, she was certain. At one point, he had even wrapped his arm around her as they sat close on the couch.

No. Henry was human. He was an Earthling.

But the Scorpiian had most likely been in his home.

She'd thought through all the angles of why it would be there. There was no reason for it to be interested in Henry. He didn't have power or influence.

The only thing that she could figure it would be looking for there was her. From her readings, she knew that it had been there after she'd visited with Henry and not before.

If it had managed to find samples of her DNA—which was pretty likely, since she and Henry had eaten a meal together and she'd probably shedded hairs on his couch—the Scorpiian would be able to take on her appearance.

Gaining access to the Department of Homeworld Security would endanger everything they were working for on Earth's behalf. And if it managed to get aboard the *Arbiter*, she shuddered to think of what it could accomplish by taking on the form of the right person at the right time.

It had already tried to manage both of those tasks before, but had been stopped by Eric and Sorca. Kira's team had been on high alert ever since, but had yet to encounter the Scorpiian again—that they knew of.

Vay's ship was locked down, so it couldn't gain entry to it. Plus, it would want to eliminate her before taking over her form. She needed to get back to her ship, but had to know that Henry was safe before she called in and told Kira...

Honestly, Vay wasn't sure what she was going to tell Kira.

But she would make it back to headquarters to tell Kira something. The scans from Vay's uniform were on maximum power and—

A blip of light appeared on her uniform's viewscreen. That couldn't be right.

One moment, there was nothing. The next, there was a human-sized lifeform a few dozen meters away. How had someone appeared so close to Vay without her sensors warning her?

Brendan called their uniforms "silver catsuits". They weren't exactly inconspicuous in the woodland setting. And there was no place for her to hide. Apparently, it was a moot point. Whoever it was had spotted her.

He immediately took off running. She wasn't sure whether she should pursue, but then her target yelled, "Hey, Sadirian. The Tau Ceti started settling down here before you. Find a different planet to exploit for resources."

A Tau Ceti? Here? She took off in pursuit. The sentient was far ahead of her, leaping over brush and ducking behind trees.

A Scorpiian might be more than she could handle, but a single Tau Ceti…

Wait. Why would a Tau Ceti be alone in a forest with no human prey nearby to feed on?

Vay needed answers, and the only way she would get them would be to catch this…whatever he was. Lucky for her, he didn't seem very coordinated.

He kept catching his coat sleeves on branches. The long white scarf he wore trailed behind him, snagging on tree limbs. One caught hard, jerking him to a stop. He made a choking noise as his legs kept going forward from his momentum, then he fell onto his back.

A huge amount of snow from the branch above dropped onto him. She reached him just as he was digging himself out, flailing as he reached the surface. She slid the power level of her wristband to its mid-range, so the blast would only stun a Tau Ceti. She could question him when he revived.

"Pheh. Pheh." He spat out snow, wiping it from his face. His eyes widened when he saw her, but probably not as wide as hers did behind the screen of her helmet.

Long straight nose, full soft lips, big brown eyes... It was Henry.

By all the stars in the void, how had they managed to run into each other again? Out here?

He looked at her wristband and raised his hands in a gesture she knew indicated surrender.

"Don't shoot," he said. "I'm an Earthling. Just an Earthling."

She opened her hands and slowly lowered them to her sides, hoping to calm him down. His chest was heaving, and his lips pulled down in a deep frown.

"How do you know about the Tau Ceti?" she said.

"I…uh… Just made it up." His gaze darted around, as if he was looking for a way to escape. "Tau Ceti is a close system. I think it's on the list of the ones who might have habitable planets."

He turned his attention back to her. "And you… You're obviously some sort of crazy person dressed up in a shiny silver catsuit. A very flattering catsuit."

He shook his head and looked away, his frown deepening.

"You called me Sadirian," Vay said.

Henry shrugged. "Just another nearby system?"

"It's not that close."

"I'm a biologist, not an astronomer." He laughed as if he'd made a joke.

"This is serious, Henry."

She saw his throat work to swallow beneath the fluffy white scarf, then he let out a foggy breath.

"How do you know my name?"

Her chest felt tight and her eyes burned. If he'd had contact with alien sentients, he would need a mind-wipe. Protocol was absolutely clear on this, and to deviate would bring down sanctions from the Coalition.

Since establishing a First Contact committee was such a high priority, Kira wouldn't risk upsetting the High Council by letting a loose end like Henry wander around Earth.

Who had been talking to him, though?

That was Vay's opening. They needed to find out what he knew and how he'd learned it. Who better to gather that information than Kira's cultural programmer? Especially since Vay had a link to Henry.

It would give her time to figure out what to do. How to protect him.

He leaned away from her, as if he was trying to escape through the earth itself. He looked terrified.

"I won't hurt you." She extended her arm to him. He stared at it for a moment, but then took it and let her help him up.

As soon as he was on his feet, he dropped her hand and started inching away. "That's nice of you to say, but it would be a lot more reassuring if I wasn't staring at my distorted reflection in your very fifties-scifi-movie-looking helmet."

"Just... Don't freak out."

"That is actually a very unsettling thing to hear from...a fellow Earthling dressed as an alien in a remote area of unpopulated forest."

She laughed and he cocked his head to the side as if she'd surprised him. With a deep breath, she tapped the side of her helmet. Its seams split open, the segments folding up on each other and nestling into the storage compartment built into the neck of her uniform.

His eyes widened. "Vay?"

She smiled and lifted her hand in a half-hearted wave.

"Hi, Henry."

"Hi." He said the word with wonder, his mouth stretching into the broad smile she was used to seeing from him. "What are you doing here?"

"I was in the neighborhood...again?"

"In a skin-tight silver catsuit." His eyebrows furrowed, but he was still smiling.

Part of her wanted to play it off as a game—to return to the banter they'd shared the day before and when they first met. But the joke was over. It was too late to go back.

"Actually, it's my uniform."

He nodded, his smile fading. "Right. Because you actually *are* an alien. Which is why you didn't know what birthdays were or Christmas or coffee or fruitcake. Or kisses."

"I actually knew what kisses were," she said. "I'd just...never participated in one."

Which it sounded like he'd noticed. She wondered if she'd done something wrong during their one and only kiss under the mistletoe. She wished that she had kissed him again yesterday, when things were simpler between them.

The wind picked up and her nose started to run. She sniffed, wishing she had some tissues or something. She didn't relish the thought of wiping her nose on the crinkly fabric of her uniform.

He quickly took off his scarf and wrapped it around her

neck. It was incredibly soft and warm.

"Here you go."

"Thanks."

His hands lingered on her shoulders. They were standing so close, she would only need to lean in a little bit to kiss him again.

Was it possible that he was okay with her being an alien? She didn't understand how he wasn't freaking out.

Something rustled in one of the bushes nearby and Henry jumped. Maybe he was internalizing his reaction. He looked past her before wrapping an arm around her shoulders and urging her to walk in the direction of his cabin.

"It seems we have some things we should probably talk about," he said. "Let's get back to the cabin where it's warmer."

"Okay." She tried to look behind them, to see what had spooked him, but didn't notice anything.

He picked up the pace, making it impossible for her to keep walking without tripping if she didn't watch where she was going. Her stomach churned with misgiving.

He knew about Sadirians. He knew about the Tau Ceti. What if he knew more? What if he *was* more? The Scorpiian.

No. There had to be another explanation. And she was going to find out what it was.

Chapter Eight

Life, in general, was weird. Being a biology teacher, Henry was aware of this. He observed it, studied it, and taught others to do the same. But his life? It had become absolutely bizarre.

He'd been adopted by a pair of space-Sasquatches from the Lyra system—who refused to take no for an answer. It was hard to be upset about that, because they were teaching him all kinds of things about the universe. Plus they were making him feel like part of a family again.

And he was walking through the forest with Vay, who had just magically reappeared in his life. And who was also an alien. An *evil* alien, if Craig and Barbara were to be believed.

"I think somebody needs to pinch me," he said.

"Why?"

"I just feel like I'm dreaming."

"I don't see how pinching you will help with that."

"It's an expression we have here on Earth."

He'd meant it as a joke at first—falling back into their "she's from another planet" game, but then realized that it was actually a perfectly reasonable thing to say.

He continued in a much more serious tone. "When someone thinks they're dreaming, they ask to be pinched so that the pain will either wake them up from the dream or prove to them that they aren't actually sleeping."

She laughed. "I'm not going to pinch you."

"It's probably for the best." After a brief pause, he said, "But you *are* Sadirian."

"Yes."

He still couldn't believe it. Not that she was an alien— hanging out with Craig and Barbara for most of the day had accustomed him to the idea of extra-terrestrial sentients walking around on his homeworld. But they had also painted a terrifying picture of Sadirians.

When her helmet had started to open, Henry knew that the person inside would look like a human. But seeing Vay's face...

Her voice pulled him from his thoughts.

"Henry, I have to ask. How do you know about us?"

"Let's wait till we're inside the cabin."

If Craig happened to be out on a walk and saw them together, Henry didn't know what would happen. He wasn't sure he could keep Vay safe, no matter how much his new—very weird—"foster parents" seemed to like him. They *hated* Sadirians.

Luckily, the cabin wasn't much farther. He hurried forward when it came into view.

The things they had said about Vay's people made

Henry's heart ache. They couldn't be true. At least, not about her. Henry needed to hear her side of things.

Once they were inside, he said, "I'll start a fire."

He hurried to the large stone fireplace that made up the entire wall to the left of the front door. Before leaving, he'd set everything up so all he had to do was strike a match and place it in a few strategic places to get the blaze going. He had wanted to be able to focus on Vay and have the cabin comfortable for her as soon as she arrived.

This wasn't what he'd pictured.

"It smells like coffee in here," she said.

"Yeah. Sorry about that." After starting the fire in the big fireplace, he headed for the potbelly stove that stood between the kitchen and living room area.

She followed him a little distance behind. "It's okay. I still like the smell."

He placed some logs in the stove. Some tea or cocoa would help calm his nerves and maybe help him feel a little more grounded. The match gave him some trouble as he tried to get it to light. Flames burst from it, catching his thumb a little too closely and burning him. The match fell harmlessly onto the stone flooring surrounding the stove.

"Are you hurt?" she asked.

"What?" He stared up at her, shaking his hand. "Oh, this. It's nothing. I'm just…trying to get the fire going." He stepped on the match to make it go out, then picked it up and threw it in with the logs before squatting down and getting out another.

"Let me help." She knelt next to him, holding up her arm.

Most of her uniform seemed to be made of a flexible fabric, but there were a few places with formed metal sections. The housing for her helmet that ringed her neck was one. Another was the wristband she was pointing at the wood in the stove.

She tapped on what looked like some etchings on the metal, then drew her finger up a line running along the side of the wristband.

"You might want to sit back," she said.

"Why?"

A bolt of light shot out of the end of her wristband as she made a fist with that hand. Henry was so startled, he fell onto his ass. The wood burst into flames.

"Are you okay?" she said.

"Yeah, I'm fine."

Except he wasn't.

Craig and Barbara might be giant, spine-fur covered, four-armed aliens, but they didn't walk around with rayguns. And Henry was betting that Vay hadn't dialed her wristband up to the maximum setting just to start a fire.

The Lyrians' ability to camouflage themselves seemed a very inadequate defense. Still, Henry didn't doubt for a second that they would attack Vay on sight. And lose.

He really needed to keep them apart. Or disarm Vay, but

in a way that would keep her safe, just in case Craig swung by the cabin and saw them together. Henry didn't want her getting hurt either.

If Craig thought Henry was entertaining another Earthling, Craig would stay out of sight. But that meant that Henry needed to get Vay out of her uniform.

"I'll make us cocoa." He scrambled to his feet, contemplating his options.

If he spilled something on her uniform, maybe she'd take it off. The cabin was still cold and the water from the reservoir on the roof would be freezing. Even a little bit of a spill on her uniform would make it uncomfortable to wear. Unless it was water-resistant.

He didn't have any better ideas. Of course, the moment he committed himself to the plan, his imagination showed him Vay slowly peeling off the skin-tight fabric.

He remembered the soft feel of her body next to his as they'd sat on the couch and talked for hours the day before. His world had seemed so much more normal then.

Letting his imagination run a little felt safer than thoughts of alien rivalries and his planet getting caught up in the middle of it.

She would need something to wear afterwards. He could picture her long legs stretching out from beneath one of his soft flannel shirts. His hands tingled at the thought of touching her. Blood started pooling in places...he really didn't want it to at the moment. He needed to focus.

Water. Cocoa. Keep Vay and Craig and Barbara safe.

The kettle sitting on the stove already had fresh water in it from the morning. He opened the cabinets above the sink and pulled out a pair of mugs, then the hot cocoa mix.

"I didn't get around to making you any yesterday," he said, "But I promise you'll like hot cocoa much more than coffee."

"I've actually already tried it. And I do."

"They have cocoa on your mothership?"

"Mothership?"

"You probably don't know that term." He poured a bit of water in the mugs, planning to offer her something to drink while he made the cocoa and maybe "tripping" as he handed it to her. "We Earthlings tell stories about extra-terrestrials. Sometimes, we reference the ship they travel on as the mothership."

"Why?"

"I'm not really sure." He'd never thought about it before. "Maybe because it takes care of the people living on it and brings them to new worlds?"

She laughed. "That's something we Sadirians would never think to call it."

"Why is that?" He was more focused on his plan than his question.

It was now or never. He started walking toward her, both mugs in his hands.

"Sadirians don't have mothers. Or parents of any kind."

Henry tripped. For real. His feet seemed to forget how to work together to carry him toward her. She reached out to catch him, bumping his arms and spilling the icy water all over both of them.

Chapter Nine

Vay reached out to catch Henry. His mass was too much for her to manage gracefully. The water he was carrying splashed out of his mugs, drenching them both. It beaded on her uniform, running off harmlessly, but it soaked through the front of Henry's shirt. It might have even hit him high enough to wet the shirt she could see underneath.

"Cold! Cold!" He set the mugs down on the counter as quickly as he could, then pulled the fabric of his shirts away from his chest.

"We need to get those off of you," she said.

Earth clothes couldn't come close to the protective qualities of her uniform and the cabin was still chilly. He had to be profoundly uncomfortable. At least the fires were starting to put off some heat.

She grabbed his elbow and pulled him toward the large fireplace just past the couch. As soon as they were in front of it, she started unbuttoning his flannel shirt.

"How do you not have parents?" he said.

"We're genetically engineered—created from genetic material from either donors or DNA banks. I guess if the donors pay to have a child created from their DNA, technically they'd be considered that citizen's parents. But even those offspring are grown in maturation chambers."

"People pay to create children in petri dishes?"

It took Vay a moment to remember what a petri dish was. "Maturation chambers are much more complex than a petri dish."

"You get what I mean, though."

She had his shirt unbuttoned and tugged it up out of his jeans, then down his arms. The white T-shirt underneath was wet all along his neck and down the front of his chest. It looked like he had on another long-sleeved shirt as well under that.

"How many layers of clothing are you wearing?" she said.

"Lots."

She pulled the T-shirt loose, then lifted the hem as far as she could. When he didn't lift his arms to help, she gave it a firm tug, glaring at him a little. He grabbed the bottom of his shirt and pulled it over his head himself.

"I'm trying not to judge your society before knowing more, but that sounds awful," he said. "Is it?"

The final layer of clothing—she hoped—was made out of thermally insulating fabric. Brendan had purchased cold weather clothing for everyone stationed on Earth to assist with the Department of Homeworld Security. The insulating layer was usually worn closest to the skin. Which meant that he was naked under it.

Her stomach started to tingle. The sensation spread quickly, dropping down through her abdomen and pooling between her legs.

If he took off this last shirt, he might get cold. She glanced at the nearby couch, noting a fuzzy blanket that was tossed over the back of it. She could wrap him up and keep him warm. And the shirt did look a little bit damp.

He should take it off. Just to be safe.

She gripped the bottom of his shirt and started to tug it free. Her gaze seemed magnetized to the latch of his jeans, and she couldn't help imagining the soft fabric of his shirt sliding against his skin.

Not all Earthlings wore undergarments. Henry might be among them. Pulling his shirt free might be stimulating his

—

"Vay?" He grabbed her hands, stopping her.

"I'm sorry."

She must have overstepped. Yes, they had shared that one kiss, and enjoyed proximity the day before, but that could have been about sharing warmth. He might not be as interested in her physically as she was in him.

At least, she assumed that was what all of these sensations flowing through her meant. It was all so new to her. He made her body respond in ways she'd never experienced before, awakening urges she wanted to explore.

"Was it awful?" he said. "Being grown in a tank and

then… What happens when you're done 'maturing'?"

"Oh."

He hadn't even been paying attention as she stripped him. She definitely hadn't made the same impression on him as he had on her.

"It was fine," she said. "Like I said, it was all we knew. Before Earth."

"But there are other sentients who still have children naturally. You have to know about those."

Who had he been *talking* to?

Even if he'd come across a rogue Tau Ceti, there was no way they would share this kind of information. Plus, their breeding program would have to strike Henry as much worse than how Sadirians made new citizens. At least with her people, there was no cannibalism of their broodmates involved.

"I don't know how you found out about all this," she said. "But it is very dangerous for you to have this knowledge."

"Dangerous for whom?" His mouth was pulled in a stern line.

"For you. If my people find out that you know all of this, they'll—"

"Order a mind-wipe. I know about the Coalition and their protocols."

She gasped. She couldn't help herself. This was so much worse than she thought.

Henry took a deep breath and let it out slowly. "But I want to hear it from you. I want to know your side of the story."

"What story? You shouldn't know any of this."

"But I do know. And since I'll probably get a mind-wipe if you report me, what's the harm in at least giving me the peace in this moment of knowing—" He clamped his mouth shut.

"Knowing what?" she said.

"Knowing that you aren't one of the bad guys."

Her heart seemed to freeze in her chest. "I'm not."

When he turned away, she reached up and gently gripped his face to try to get him to look at her again. He stared at the shining material of her gloves, his mouth forming that line again. She wanted his smile. The openness that he'd shared with her the night they met.

She stepped away from him, tapping commands into her wristband as quickly as she could. As soon as she heard it release, she snapped open the compartment for her helmet, then unsealed her uniform.

"What are you doing?"

"I'm showing you exactly who I am."

She had her uniform off in seconds. Gloves, boots, all of it. She wadded it up in a ball and tossed it behind the couch, leaving her standing in front of Henry in just the black mini top and form-fitting shorts the Coalition provided female soldiers to wear beneath their uniforms.

Even that was too much—a link to them she couldn't stand. She started to peel off her undergarments, but Henry stepped forward and grabbed her wrists, stopping her.

"Vay."

The room was blurry. Her eyes had filled with tears. She pulled her arms free from him and wiped them away.

"This. This is who I am. V-21-b3. Twenty-first embryo of batch three from the V unit. Cultural programmer. One of the most valueless functions in our society. They don't call us anthropologists or social scientists. I'm a cultural programmer. Do you know why we're called that?"

"No." Henry's voice was barely above a whisper.

"Because we don't study cultures to learn ways to improve our own or even simply for the sake of expanding our knowledge and understanding of each other like you do on Earth. We study them to figure out the best ways to destroy them. To *program* them so that they follow Coalition law. That was my entire reason for existing before I came to Earth."

"And what is it now?"

"I've been tasked with learning more about how so many different cultures exist on Earth simultaneously. How they manage to interact and deal with differences. We're hoping that we can present a case to the High Council that will show them there are other ways—better ways—of ruling the galaxy."

"Why do I feel like there's a 'but' coming?"

"If they don't listen, my colleagues and I will most likely face disciplinary action for overstepping our orders. Maybe even be mind-wiped ourselves. They'll put us into reprogramming pods and turn us into whatever kinds of soldiers they want us to be."

She started to tremble, thinking of that very likely future. "Henry, I don't want to go back to that."

He grasped her face firmly and pulled her toward him. Liquid fire seemed to pour along her skin as his lips touched hers. The kiss wasn't tentative like their first had been. He claimed her mouth, his tongue sliding along her lips until she opened for him.

She wrapped her arms around his waist, pulling him closer. His warmth seeped into her, bone-deep. Stars, she'd never felt anything like it.

Slowly, he ended the kiss and shifted back a bit.

"Sorry," he said.

"For what?"

"Losing control."

"Never apologize for kissing me. Especially like that."

He chuckled, running his hands lightly down her arms. "Vay, I don't understand everything that's going on. But I'm going to do my best to help you."

"I know."

It was strange to be so sure of him already, but she was certain he would help in any way he could. She just had to be sure he didn't endanger himself by trying.

Chapter Ten

"You must be freezing," Henry said.

The fires were starting to heat up the cabin, but there was no way the tiny strips of fabric Vay was wearing could be keeping her warm. His slightly-damp thermal shirt was barely keeping him from shivering.

He led her to the couch, wrapping her in the blanket he always kept there.

"Thanks." She pulled him down next to her, holding onto his hand tightly.

"We're going to figure this out."

"It's not your burden. I'm sorry I was so upset a moment ago, but I can handle it. Really."

"I believe you. But you don't have to handle it alone."

"I'm not alone. There's a whole team assigned to Earth at the moment."

"I don't know if that's reassuring or not." He shrugged, and said, "At least they're friends of yours. That says something about them."

"Something good, I hope." She gave him a tentative smile.

"Yes."

"We're setting up a First Contact committee with several Earthlings on it. We hope to establish good relations between our people."

"Any chance they need a high school biology teacher with an interest in—" He stopped himself before saying, 'cryptozoology'.

As much as he hated to admit it, letting her know about that side of him could endanger Craig and Barbara. Bigfoot was the most well-known cryptid. He didn't want Vay to figure out his source of information was a Lyrian.

"I'm not sure," Vay said. "I would ask, but if they find out about you..."

"They'll probably insist on a mind-wipe."

"If I don't tell anyone, maybe they won't discover you. But you'd have to promise not to tell anyone what you've learned."

He laughed. "Who would believe me?"

She arched an eyebrow at him and frowned.

"But more importantly," he said, "I won't tell anyone anything in the first place. I promise."

Her lips quirked back up into a smile. Lips he had recently kissed. And she had kissed him back.

It was hard not to think about how little she was wearing under the blanket.

"Are you sure you don't want to put your uniform back on?"

She shuddered. "No, I'm fine."

"You don't seem fine."

"I'd rather be cold than wear that. I hate it."

Henry was surprised at the vehemence of her words.

"It's not that bad," he said. "I mean, it's a little 1950's scifi cliché, but—"

She broke in before he could finish his thought. "Do you know how often we have to wear our uniforms? Always. That's the kind of existence I have to look forward to when I go back. The only time we can take them off is for bodily eliminations. And those only happen every couple of days, thanks to the regen beds and the specially formulated 'food' they make us eat." She made sarcastic air quotes when she said the word. "With all the development effort they put into our nutrient bricks, you'd think they would have some flavor or texture, but they don't."

"At least it's not—"

"Please don't make a Soylent Green joke."

Henry let out a short laugh. "How do you know about Soylent Green?"

"My commanding officer's husband, Brendan, is a self-proclaimed geek."

"Husband. So, you guys get married. And sometimes to Earthlings, unless you also have geeks among your kind."

She grinned at that. "Several of my colleagues have fallen in love with Earthlings and pair-bonded with them."

A sharp spike of dread hit his system. Her life sounded

terrible, and he could imagine her trying to escape it by any means necessary. He was trying very hard not to be suspicious of her interest in him.

She was gorgeous, smart, funny... He wasn't used to someone like her being attracted to someone like him.

"Vay, I have to ask. You aren't looking for some Earthling to...pair-bond with so you can—"

"Please don't make a 'Gray card' joke. And that's not what this is about."

He felt his eyebrows rise up his forehead and had trouble bringing them back down. "Brendan again?"

She shook her head. "Evelyn. She was the first Earthling to pair-bond with one of us. She told me she initially had similar concerns about General Serath's interest in her. But with Scorpiians—what you call Grays —operating on Earth, I'd rather not joke about them."

"Grays are real? And on Earth?" His forehead was going to cramp at this rate.

"It's not a good thing. They're shape-shifting assassins who can take on the form of anyone whose DNA they've sampled."

"Cool," Henry said.

She arched an eyebrow at him.

He feigned a stern expression. "I mean, that's terrible. Very frightening."

It actually was, if he let himself think about it. He wanted to keep his focus on Vay—on this moment they were sharing.

She looked away briefly, then said, "I was actually a little concerned for about a nanosecond that maybe you were…"

"What, a Gray? Me?" He laughed and shook his head. "I promise I am not a shape-shifting alien assassin. Or an alien of any kind. At least, as far as Earth is concerned."

"Actually…"

His heartbeat picked up. "Vay. I'm not an alien. Right?"

"Technically, you kind of are. I mean, your people have been on Earth for so long, the Coalition considers you Earthlings, but humans are actually descended from a Sadirian colony ship that crashed here millennia ago."

"But that… The fossil record…" His brain stalled.

Craig and Barbara hadn't mentioned any of this. But then, they probably wanted to distance Henry from the Sadirians as much as possible in their minds.

"The hominids evolving at the time were following a very similar path," Vay said. "Certain planetary environments tend to favor similar results."

He could think of several examples of that on Earth— birds that evolved forms best suited to their ecosystem that were almost identical to different species in other regions. But thinking about that sort of thing on the level of humanity made his brain stall again.

She leaned forward and kissed him, and his thoughts stopped altogether. It wasn't like the tentative kiss they'd shared on Christmas Eve. Her mouth moved against his, assertive, demanding. She buried her fingers in his hair.

Whatever else was going on, there was something happening between them. A spark that neither could deny. He gave in to the pleasure rippling through him, pushing her back on the couch and covering her with his body. They were the same species. Which meant they were biologically compatible—hopefully.

He should probably check.

Shifting his lips to her neck, he trailed a line of kisses toward her ear, then said, "We can do this, right? Earthlings and Sadirians?"

"Yes." Her voice was a breathy moan. "Just tell me what to do."

That was weird. Surely she knew what would be involved. Unless she'd never...

He pushed himself up on his elbows, a different kind of pleasure warming him as he saw her flushed cheeks and heavy-lidded eyes.

"You've done this before, right? Maybe not with Earthlings, but with other Sadirians?"

Her eyes became a bit more focused—and shuttered. "I have. But we do things differently."

"Different how?" All sorts of scenarios ran through his head. He tried to tame his imagination before it completely extinguished his ardor.

"When Sadirians have sex, we use a drug called

Coupling. It handles pretty much everything for us. Arousal, climax, aftereffects."

"That sounds like...no fun at all."

She laughed. "It's a *little* fun. But not like this. I stopped using it with a partner years ago. It has about the same effect solo."

"You even use it by yourself?"

"*Most* Sadirians use it by themselves. It's designed to satisfy our biological urges. Interacting with a partner while using it is sort of looked down upon."

He laughed and shook his head. "That's kind of the opposite of a lot of Earthlings. But if you've never...'explored yourself', how do you know what you enjoy?"

"I was kind of hoping to figure that out with you."

Oh boy.

Meeting Vay and being with her like this already felt like some kind of miracle. What she wanted to experience with him, though—her first real physical intimacy—was sacred ground.

He rose from the couch, pulling her after him. He grabbed the blanket and wrapped it over her shoulders.

"I don't understand," she said.

"It sounds like that drug put your body on autopilot. I want to be sure that you can focus on this experience completely."

"Okay."

He led her to the fireplace, where the stones were already radiating heat. Swallowing hard, he took the blanket from her and laid it on the floor. Then he slid his fingertips under the hem of her sports bra and lifted it over her breasts.

He tried not to stare as she shimmied out of it. He really tried.

Her breasts were perfect. Full and round, with rose-colored nipples that he couldn't wait to taste.

But he would.

He turned her around and lifted her hand to the mantel. "Hold onto this."

She did as he asked, looking back at him over her shoulder. The trust she was showing... He would live up to it. He was going to help her, no matter what it took. Starting with this. An introduction to her own body.

"Many Earthlings explore their bodies to learn what they do and don't like," he said.

"Explore how?"

He stepped up behind her, his heart pounding. He was already so hard. His balls were aching. He took a moment to adjust himself and her eyes widened.

"Don't worry." He smiled at her. "This time I'm keeping the focus entirely on you."

"I don't know what that means."

"Then let me show you."

She smiled at him, then turned back toward the fire. He

heard her let out a nervous breath. A soft orange glow bathed her skin. He wanted to see more of it. And it would help him to help her.

He hooked his fingers in the waistband of the tight shorts she was wearing, then slid them down her long legs. When they'd reached her ankles, she stepped out of them. He was at eye-level with her ass. He could imagine standing and grabbing her hips and driving himself into her.

But not yet. Not. Yet.

He ran his hands up her legs as he slowly stood, then along her sides. When he reached her breasts, he cupped them firmly, kneading their softness. She sucked in a breath and jerked back, but he was right there to keep her steady. He pressed her firmly against his chest, massaging her breasts the entire time.

"Do you feel that?" he said. "The weakness in your knees. The fluttering in your stomach. Anticipation. Desire."

She leaned against his chest, nuzzling his cheek. "I feel it."

He rolled her nipples gently between his fingers, till they tightened. Vay arched her back, pushing her ass against his dick.

This was going to be harder than he thought. He wanted to thrust against her. But he didn't want to distract her from what she was feeling from and within her own body.

"Cygnus X. That feels so good."

"So good you're thinking about a black hole?"

She laughed. "It's a phrase that indicates strong emotion."

"We're only getting started."

"What are you going to do?" Her voice was breathless.

"What are *you* going to do. I'm only here to help."

Her hair was short enough that he could move it aside by nuzzling her neck, and as soon as he'd bared her skin, he nipped it gently. She pressed back against him, shifting her ass in a maddening way. He placed his left hand next to hers on the mantel, then lifted her right with his and set it on her stomach.

He pressed his dick against her harder, felt it start to pulse a bit. He couldn't believe how worked up she was getting him. It was time to return the favor.

He guided her hand down her stomach, till they reached the soft curls at the apex of her legs. He sucked the skin of her neck, tonguing her flesh as he lined up her fingers with her slit.

Apparently, kissing had excited her more than he thought. She was already slick. He entwined their fingers, circling her clit, flicking it, rubbing all along the length of her.

"Henry…"

She moaned, spreading her legs to give them better access. His heart was hammering in his chest. He had never wanted anyone so badly. If he wasn't careful, he was going to go off in his pants.

He had plans, though. So many plans. Things he'd imagined doing to and with her during the time they'd been apart. But he had to last through this for them both to experience even more.

He pressed his dick against her ass, trying to focus completely on her as he pushed on her hand, guiding her fingers deeper, into her core. She gasped, but he didn't let up. In and out, rhythmically pumping her hand with his— slowly, letting her savor every impulse from her nerve endings. She took over for him, alternating between deep thrusts with her fingers and quick swirls around her clit.

"That's it," he murmured in her ear. "It's your body. Figure out what you like."

And then hopefully she'd let him do the same to her.

"I don't know what... I don't know how to climax on my own." She looked over at him, eyes soft with pleasure, lips still full from their kisses.

He covered her hand with his again, pressing her hips harder against his swollen dick. Imagining what it would be like to part her flesh and bury himself in her. The thought almost set him off again. Maybe it would help her too.

"Imagine me buried inside of you."

He whispered the words against her ear, then nipped it as he started to thrust against her. Pulling her fingers up to her clit, he moved them in a few quick circles until she had taken over on her own.

"Only I'd be going deeper." He slid one of his fingers into her core, pumping it as he thrust against her.

"Faster." He slid a second finger in.

She let out a groan and rose up on her toes, as if she was trying to position his dick to plow into her. He was throbbing so hard, about to go off any second. He wanted this to be about her, but his body was reacting as if everything he was saying was true.

"Harder." He slid a third finger in deep, pumping them relentlessly, thrusting against her in time with his movements.

He felt her core spasm around his hand, pulling on his fingers, milking them. He pressed against her clit with the heel of his hand as he kept going, wanting this climax to be one she would never forget.

She threw her head back and screamed, "Stars!"

He pressed himself to her as hard as he could, fingers still buried deep as her body calmed against him—willing his own to calm as well. He wanted this moment to last.

And then he wanted more. More moments like this.

He wanted more time.

Chapter Eleven

Vay was still reeling from her body seeming almost to unmake itself through the searing orgasm Henry had shared with her. The knowledge that her body was capable of giving her more of this pleasure without the assistance of Coupling was incredible. And if it felt that good on her own, she couldn't imagine how much better it would be with a partner.

"Henry—"

She could still feel the fullness of his member pressed against her ass, but he'd let go of his hold on her. He was moving around behind her, getting something out of his pocket.

"I forget my hat, I forget my gloves, but I always have my wallet with me, even when hiking through the forest."

He tossed his wallet on the floor, finally shifting back from her. She heard him unzip his pants, and the rustle of fabric as he pulled them open. Was he not going to undress?

Part of her wanted to experience his skin against hers. Another part wanted him inside of her immediately. The latter desire increased in strength as the velvet skin of his shaft rubbed against her hip as he moved.

She craned her neck to glance at him over her shoulder. He was holding a small metal packet between his teeth. He tore it open and pulled a small piece of plastic or something from it. He unrolled the material down his shaft.

A condom. She remembered reading about them. He grabbed her hips, pausing when their gazes met.

"Are you sure you want to do this?" he said. "I mean, with me?"

She wrapped her arm around his neck, pulling him close for a kiss. She could feel him prodding against her flesh.

"Absolutely," she said.

He let out a sigh, then kissed her again, his tongue sliding between her lips. One of his hands found her breast again, while the other delved between her legs, as if he hadn't gotten his fill of feeling her in that intimate way.

He shifted his hips, angling them beneath her as he released her mouth. She could feel the tip of him pressing against her core. Turning back to the fire, she gripped the mantel with both hands to steady herself.

Henry slid into her, slowly, his fingers digging into her hips as he let out a low groan. A matching sound escaped from her chest. He was stretching her, filling her.

Heat and the purest experience of *sensation* flooded her body, generated from where they were connected. Finally, she felt his pelvis pressing against her ass.

All of him was within her. All of him.

The thought sent another wave of tingling stimulation over her skin. He leaned back, releasing her hips, but keeping himself buried inside her, then pulled his shirt off and tossed it away.

"I want to feel more of you." He leaned forward, so that his chest touched her back.

Henry's warmth seeped into her. More of him—his energy—soaking into her. Then his hands were on her again. Kneading her breast, circling her clitoris. She felt a deep pulsing throb within her.

"Was that your climax?" she asked.

"What?"

Henry laughed, and she could feel the vibration through their body. They were connected everywhere, it seemed.

"No," he said. "I'm trying to calm myself down before moving—to *avoid* my climax. Well, put it off for a bit, at least. There's so much I want to experience with you."

A pang shot through her that nearly equaled in pain what he was giving her in physical pleasure. There was so much she wanted to experience with him, too. So much they would never have time to explore together.

She needed to be distracted from those thoughts. She needed more of him, of this.

"Henry, please…"

His hands moved to her hips, his grip strong. Slowly, he

pulled himself from her almost completely, then slid back in. The friction sent shooting tendrils of pleasure through her, like sparks lighting up every nerve-ending.

Again, he pulled himself out, then thrust back inside of her. As he'd promised, he started to move faster, landing harder. She clenched her fingertips onto the mantel to hold herself up. His pelvis slapped against her ass as his pace increased, his body ramming into her like a piston.

The sparks along her nerves started coalescing into a flame that burned white-hot, filling her body, flooding through her. Her heart seemed to stop for a moment, everything stilling, until it burst through her awareness in a cascading torrent of sensation. The flames coursed through her body, energizing every cell, every molecule. She'd never felt such a pure connection to another.

Henry cried out her name as his pounding thrusts reached a frenzied level. She felt his shaft pulsing within her, resonating with the aftereffects of her own climax and keeping her in that blissful state for that much longer.

He finally stopped, buried as deeply within her as he could reach, his chest pressed against her back and his hands wrapped around her waist. She felt him rest his head on her shoulder, a shudder passing through him.

"That was incredible," she said.

"I wholeheartedly agree."

"Thank you."

"You are most welcome."

He laughed and she felt him slide from her body. The absence was disorienting. She tried not to think about how his absence would affect her when he was gone from her life entirely.

He turned her to face him, pulling her against his chest. The fire was warm, as was he.

"How long do we have?" he said.

So, he was thinking along the same lines as she was. It was hard to ignore the reality of their situation. But she could try.

"We have today. Maybe tomorrow."

He sucked in a quick breath, and his eyes seemed to glitter in the firelight. He pulled her close and pressed his lips to her forehead. For a long moment, he left them there.

"Let's not waste it," he said. "Any of it."

She nodded, her throat too tight to speak. He lifted her chin so that he could look into her eyes.

"Vay. Every moment with you is a gift."

She let out the breath she hadn't known she was holding, then wrapped her arms around his neck and held him tight.

There had to be a way they could share more of this. She could start the arduous bureaucratic process that would enable her to stay. But that might endanger General Serath's efforts to have the First Contact committee recognized.

She could ask Henry to come with her. He might just

agree, if he felt even half as strongly toward her as she felt toward him. But she cared about him too much to ask it of him.

She could fake her own death...

Her ideas were getting more desperate—and ridiculous. She'd never be able to pull it off. She'd be found, disciplined, and Henry would receive a mind-wipe.

Her mind was still reeling, eating up the precious time she had in Henry's arms. She needed to focus on what she had in each moment. And maybe while she was doing her scans back at her ship she could figure out a way they could be together.

Chapter Twelve

The light streaming in through the windows was starting to gain a tint of orange. Normally, Henry loved the sunset views from the cabin.

His life had become anything but normal.

The sun setting meant that Vay would be leaving soon. She should be back at her ship before dark. Her uniform would probably keep her warm and help her see, though. Maybe they could have a bit more time together.

He'd do anything for more time with her.

Her people valued love. They had to if it was possible for them to pair-bond with Earthlings. And if others could do it, why couldn't they?

It might have seemed sudden from an external view, but it wasn't. His feelings for her had been building since their chance encounter on Christmas Eve. This was the real thing. He was sure of it.

His dad often talked to Henry about how he and Henry's mom became a couple. It was love at first sight on dad's part. His dad had winked as he said, "You mother took a little convincing." But he explained that their future together had been worth fighting for.

Henry would fight for his future with Vay. Even if it was complicated by the fact that she was an alien.

Unless that could make it easier...

She seemed to hate her life with the Coalition. From how controlling they sounded, Henry doubted that they would just let her go. But maybe she could escape. All she'd need was a little help. And he happened to know a pair of Lyrians who were adept at avoiding the Coalition. He just had to convince them to use their skills on Vay's behalf.

Sure, because they love Sadirians so much.

They might not love Sadirians, but they seemed really taken with Henry—a feeling that he couldn't deny was mutual. It was the weirdest thing, but hanging out with them and talking and laughing had felt like family. Craig had even said as much, and Barbara had called Henry "nestling" before he left.

Vay shifted closer against him under the huge pile of blankets he'd heaped in front of the fireplace screen. Her legs were entwined with his and her arm draped over his chest. He kissed the top of her head, and she let out a contented cooing sound.

If he was Craig and Barbara's family, then so was Vay. Henry had to convince them to help her.

He wasn't actually sure she'd welcome their help. The Lyrians' hatred of Sadirians might not be one-sided, and knowing that in advance seemed like a good idea. Coming at the matter head-on didn't seem wise, so he started with a different line of questioning.

"Tell me about the Tau Ceti."

Vay laughed. "I thought you already knew about them, from your mysterious source of information."

"I want to hear your perceptions of them."

"Okay." She was silent for a moment, her fingertips trailing soothing circles over his chest. "They're amphibians. They evolved from something similar to frogs. Their genetic engineers modified them to look more like Sadirians and they can now stay away from water for a long time. The best specimens are difficult to differentiate from us, but most have telltale characteristics that set them apart. Narrow eyes, wide mouths."

"Great."

And Craig had said that Barbara comparing Henry to a Tau Ceti was a compliment?

"You know why they're on Earth, right?" she said.

"No."

Craig and Barbara had covered so much ground with Henry. Since he didn't really know much about all of these new species in the first place, he didn't know what questions to ask. The galaxy was much more populous than he'd dreamed.

When Vay didn't continue, he prompted her. "I take it from your silence that it isn't a good reason."

"It isn't. But they're not killing anyone, at least. That

we know of."

A chill swept over him. "The fact that you're opening with that is not as reassuring as you might be going for."

"Sorry. The Tau Ceti have modified their forms further so that they have retractable fangs that they use to siphon blood out of humans. They strip the blood of certain chemicals—oxytocin, dopamine—and return it with a chemical agent that causes memory loss."

The chill turned to nausea.

"That's awful," he said.

"I agree."

"Let's talk about another species. You said there were Grays on Earth. You called them Scorpiians?"

This time, she was the one who shivered. She put her arm back across his chest, hugging him close.

"Now I'm really freaking out. They're worse than the Tau Ceti?"

"So much worse," she said.

"You said they're shapeshifters. All they need is some DNA to take on another form. Does it have to be a being with similar biomass?"

"Nobody knows the extent of their abilities for certain. They're very secretive."

He wondered if he had her distracted enough to bring up Craig and Barbara. His palms were starting to sweat. With her head resting on his chest, she could probably hear his heart rate increasing.

"Let's see," he said. "What other systems are nearby that we've found possibly habitable planets for? There's Cygnus."

"Cygnus-1 is populated. There's a black hole nearby, which causes gravity fluctuations that actually protect the planet from too much Coalition interference. Plus, they've evolved to have incredible strength and speed. Their skin is incredibly hard as well—almost like stone."

"They sound like gargoyles."

"I haven't come across that word yet."

"They're decorative stone statues that we have legends about coming to life and moving around. You should look them up." This was the perfect segue into asking about the Lyrians. "Speaking of legends... I'm starting to wonder how many of our legendary creatures are actually alien visitors. Take Bigfoot, for example."

Vay snickered. "Who?"

"Bigfoot. The Sasquatch. It's a really tall, hairy creature that roams through the woods. They leave big footprints, hence the name."

"I was wondering."

"Most legends say they're brown, but some people think that the Yeti might also be a form of Sasquatch, and those are white..." He let his voice trail off, hoping she would fill in the rest.

"Sounds like a Lyrian."

Yes!

"Oh? What are those like?" He hoped he was doing a good enough job keeping his voice calm.

Her grip loosened on his chest. At least she didn't seem to be afraid of them.

"They're tall and have spines that I've heard are really soft. They even look like fur. The spines are colorless, but appear white due to how they refract light. Lyrians can actually bend light around themselves at will, giving them a natural cloaking mechanism. It helps them with their criminal activities."

"Come on, they can't all be criminals."

"Of course not. But the ones we encounter are almost all involved in something that goes against Coalition law."

"The Coalition has sounded pretty crappy, from everything you've told me."

"Well, yeah, but I'm talking about thievery and smuggling."

His hopes of Vay getting along with Craig and Barbara started to tailspin. "It sounds like you don't think highly of them."

"There's a saying on Sadr-4. Lyrians have four arms to help them steal."

"Okay, I get it. Let's…move on."

It wasn't just that she was confirming his fears about her people's opinion of Lyrians. Henry couldn't stand to hear her badmouthing people he respected and trusted, even after talking to them for such a little while.

If only she could get to know them as he had. All they wanted was to help other sentients. He was sure they would help her, once they understood the situation.

"Henry..."

When she didn't continue, he said, "Yes?"

"Where did you get that scarf?"

Crap.

He didn't want to tell her—on many levels. He didn't want to think about it himself, even though the scarf really was the warmest and softest thing he'd ever worn. And it was sort of a sweet gesture.

Lots of humans wore clothing made from animal fur. The donors just usually...weren't sentient. Or so insistent about it. And they didn't pluck out their fur and weave it into a scarf right in front of you.

"Henry, you haven't been talking to a Lyrian, have you?"

"No."

Technically, he hadn't. "I've been talking to two."

Chapter Thirteen

Vay pushed herself up on Henry's chest so that she could look him in the eye. She had to be sure that he was serious about what he was saying. But how would he even know to make a joke about such a thing?

"They're really nice," he said.

"That's insane. Do you know how dangerous Lyrians are?"

"I do."

"Obviously you don't, or you wouldn't have associated with them."

He sat up and shifted away from her. The motion chilled her in a way that went beyond the physical absence of his body heat.

"I'm going to give you a pass on that one, since I'm assuming that your uber-controlling government has given you false information about them."

"Henry…"

"Have you ever talked to a Lyrian? Just sat down and had a conversation? Maybe played some cards. Sang some songs."

"Sadirians don't do those sorts of things."

"I know. But Lyrians do. Did the Coalition include that aspect of their culture in your training on their civilization, or did they focus on the whole 'if they get mad, they tear your arms off' thing? Because yes, they do that—which is really disturbing. But their physiology is so different than ours it means something totally different among their kind. And they don't do that to other species. Usually."

Her heart was thundering. The Lyrians would only have given Henry a scarf made from their fur—one of the most sought after and precious commodities their planet offered, and one they very seldom willingly shared—if they considered him kin. Which meant their protective instincts would be fully engaged.

Anyone they perceived as a threat to him would definitely fall outside of that "usually" addendum about them not pulling off other species' arms. She didn't want Henry to learn about their violent tendencies by watching them tear her apart.

And she really didn't want to be torn apart.

"Henry, this is—"

"They can help you."

She let out a laugh before she could stop herself. "A Lyrian is not about to help a Sadirian. They hate us."

"From what you've said, the feeling is pretty mutual."

All the warmth had left his tone. His lips were pulled in a tight line—lips that she had so recently felt caressing her skin. She wanted his laughter back.

Most of all, she wanted him safe.

"There are some beautiful aspects of their culture," she said. "But there are also records of attacks. Plus, they're notorious smugglers."

"I believe it."

She was so stunned by the revelation that she just stared at him. She couldn't think of what to say.

"I absolutely believe Lyrians have attacked Sadirians," he said. "And that Sadirians have also attacked them. But without having full information on what happened in those circumstances, I'm withholding judgment—on both parties. Maybe you should give that a try."

Her eyes filled with tears. He had obviously become attached to the Lyrians, too. And he'd assimilated their hatred for Sadirians—for her.

"This was a mistake," she said. "I shouldn't have come here."

When she turned from him and tried to stand, he grabbed her arm, holding her in place.

"This wasn't a mistake. Please don't think that. Never think that." He pulled her close against his chest, smoothing her hair with one hand as he held her tight. "I'm sorry. I guess I'm just...protective of them."

She let out a small laugh, wiping at her eyes as she leaned back to look at him again while they spoke. "I don't know what to think about this."

"Just open your mind to the possibility that what you

believe about them might be wrong. Or at least skewed in favor of the Coalition."

That wasn't hard to do, actually. Everything the High Council did was skewed in favor of the Coalition.

Moons, she'd reacted just the way she'd been trained—had jumped to the conclusions they planted in her brain in her initial programming sessions. After everything she'd learned about the Coalition, everything she'd seen with her own eyes, she knew better.

And there was also so much beauty to the Lyrian culture. Their intense love of family, their incredible sense of community.

"You're right," she said. "The Coalition is terrible to sentients who can't—or won't—conform to Sadirian standards."

"From what you've told me, they're not even good to their own people."

She nodded, her mind trying to wrap itself around this new—and stunning—information.

"The best lies are the ones that have a bit of truth in them," he said. "Lyrians do get mad and tear off each others' arms—or even their own sometimes."

"Why would they do that?"

"If one of their arms is damaged beyond their ability to heal it, they'll pull it off. And if that throws off their balance, sometimes they do the same to the one opposite it, knowing that both will grow back."

"That's deeply disturbing."

"For you and I, it's alien."

She arched an eyebrow at him.

"Let me rephrase that," he said. "It's outside of our experience."

The smile she loved so much pulled at the corners of his mouth. Warmth spread through her chest at the sight.

"What about the smuggling? The thievery?"

"Another misinterpretation," he said. "At least, in the case of my friends. Earth's biomes are incredibly diverse. We have ecosystems that match dozens of inhabited planets—planets that have singular environments."

"Earth's diversity is part of why it has preservation status. It's an alluring target for sentients who want to exploit your resources."

"They aren't here to exploit us. They're gathering seeds."

The misgiving that she was fighting against came back full force. "Henry, that is a serious crime in the Coalition. How is that not stealing from your planet?"

"They aren't stealing. I'm giving them what they need," Henry said. "After talking to them and learning about their mission, I'll help them any way I can."

"You don't have the authority."

"Who are they going to ask for permission? Your government? Mine? I can go to any garden shop and buy what they need with my own resources."

"But that's what this is all about. Resources. Earth isn't capable of supplying resources to every planet with sentient inhabitants who feel slighted by the Coalition."

"Slighted? We're talking about worlds that have been completely stripped of what they need to sustain life. People that are now dependent on the Coalition for survival."

"People who traded their resources—"

"Who made a mistake. A huge, terrible mistake. Some of them hundreds or even thousands of years ago. And they're still suffering."

"You can't damage your own planet to save theirs."

"I don't have to. All Craig and Barbara need are a few samples of each specimen, and they can replicate them to distribute to planets in need. They just need the genetic templates to use as a baseline for the worlds they're helping."

"Craig and Barbara?"

Henry shrugged. "Those are their chosen Earth names."

Their efforts almost sounded like what Brendan's sister, Paige, was proposing. She had left with Khel to try to convince the High Council to let her use her knowledge of environmental science to repair the damage to worlds in the same type of situation Henry was describing.

"They're just trying to help other sentients to lead better lives," he said.

That didn't sound right. Lyrians had always been

described as mercenary. They were the Earth equivalent of pirates. But now that she was thinking about it, she didn't remember hearing stories about Lyrians selling anything for profit. Her training mostly said that they were focused on "leading planets away from the Coalition's care".

She let out a breath that seemed to empty her as she actually felt her paradigm shift.

"Are you okay?" Henry said.

"Yeah. I'm just…processing all of this."

"I don't mean to heap more on you, but there's a time factor here."

"Are they on a deadline or something?"

"No, but you are."

Now she was really confused. Although, looking out the window, the sun was getting ready to set. She had maybe thirty minutes of daylight left.

"Vay, I have to ask you something that's very important."

"Okay."

"Do you want to go back to the Coalition?"

Her blood seemed to still in her veins. She couldn't breathe, couldn't dare to hope. But if he was thinking of offering her an escape, was it because he felt sympathy for her, or something else? Something deeper?

"I don't," she said, at last. "But I will. To help your planet. To help you. If I don't go back, they'll search for me."

He shook his head. "The Lyrians can help you. Like you said, they *are* smugglers. Just good-guy smugglers."

She almost managed a laugh, but it came out as more of a pained sigh. "There's more going on with Earth than you know."

"Like the Tau Ceti? Centaurans?"

Vay scoffed. "Your friends really do know a lot. But do they know about the Scorpiian?"

"They didn't mention any Grays. I'm assuming they know about the bugs."

She laughed, which was kind of amazing, given what they were talking about. Henry had that power over her. It was its own kind of magic. But this was too serious a matter for Vay to let herself get distracted.

"I'm talking about the bounty hunter that tried to infiltrate both the Department of Homeworld Security and the *Arbiter* itself before it left orbit," she said.

"They might have thought it was too scary for me." He shrugged. "I tried to explain that I'm an adult, but when they found out that my parents had died, they insisted on adopting me as their nestling."

"Your parents?"

He looked away. "Just before Christmas."

Her breath rushed out of her. That was what he'd been dealing with when they'd met. When he talked about letting go of his family's traditions, she'd had no idea what he must have been going through.

"Henry—"

"Yeah, Craig and Barbara were pretty upset about it, too." He smiled at her, but his eyes glittered and she could see thin lines around his mouth. as if he was in pain. "They think I need them. And I guess I kind of do. They're the only family I have now. Except for you."

Chapter Fourteen

From the way Vay's eyes widened, Henry was pretty sure she understood what he meant by that. Just in case he wasn't being clear, he figured he should tell her in his own Earthling way.

"I love you, Vay. I have since we met on Christmas Eve. I dream about you at night and think of you all the time. But not in a stalker-y way." He shook his head. "I'm not saying this well."

"I love you, too." She squeezed his hand, giving him the brightest smile he'd ever seen.

His heart was thundering in his chest. "Does that mean the same thing—"

She leaned in and kissed him. Her lips were like velvet. She ran her tongue across his mouth and he opened himself to her, met her in a dance that they'd been practicing all day, but seemed to have reached a new level with this. They were in love.

When she ended the kiss, she said, "It means I dream about you, too. I think about you. I wonder what you're doing, what you're thinking. I sleep with the fruitcake you gave me under my pillow every night."

He arched an eyebrow and smiled. "Okay, that does sound a little stalker-y. And messy."

"It's in a stasis pod, so it's not messy."

"I guess that's a good thing."

She let out a short laugh. "And I don't know what 'stalker-y' means."

"It's not a real word. And I shouldn't have mentioned it. It's someone who has an unhealthy attachment to another person. They follow them around, which we call stalking, because they want something from them. Recognition, control, to make them afraid—"

Vay's eyes widened suddenly. She dropped his hands and leapt to her feet. "Where's my uniform?"

"Behind the couch." Henry rose as well. Something in the intensity of her movements made his stomach sink. He grabbed his own clothes and started dressing as quickly as he could. "What's going on?"

She was already slipping the silver material on, not bothering with her undergarments. "I have to go."

"Is it because the sun is setting? If we go to Craig and Barbara—"

"That's where I'm going."

"Then I definitely need to go with you."

"No, you have to stay." She stopped and looked around, her eyebrows furrowing as she let out what sounded disturbingly like a groan of despair. "But it isn't safe for you here, either."

He'd finished putting on his clothes and ran to the door. His boots were still wet, but he started putting them on anyway.

"Vay, you're freaking me out. What's happening?"

"Scorpiians are sometimes smugglers, too. They're known to trade in forbidden items of high value."

"Like a space black market?"

"I'm unfamiliar with that term."

"Forget it."

She pulled on her gloves and checked the ring of metal around her neck that housed her helmet. Then she powered up the wristband attached to her uniform.

Henry's fear intensified. He pulled on his coat and grabbed the scarf that Craig had made him—from his own fur—then hesitated for a moment. All the hair on Henry's arms suddenly stood on end and his stomach seemed to turn to a chunk of ice in his middle.

"Craig told me that his pelt can be used as an ultimate cloaking device, even if he's not in it," Henry said.

Vay froze. Slowly, she looked over at him.

"You tracked the Scorpiian here. To this area. It isn't…" He could barely force out the words. "It isn't after them, is it? Craig and Barbara?"

"Henry…"

That was all he needed to hear. He threw open the door, wrapping the scarf around his neck as he ran toward their ship. He could hear Vay's footsteps behind him.

"You can't know for sure," he said, between gasps.

Vay wasn't winded at all. "I tracked the Scorpiian to your cabin. I didn't understand why it was interested in you, but if it's trying to get close to the Lyrians, using your appearance would be a perfect way to do it."

It must have been watching them—watching their ship. How had it even known where to look?

Craig had said he'd been watching Henry. Maybe Craig wasn't always using his ability to conceal himself while doing so. Henry said a silent prayer that it wasn't his fault that the Scorpiian had found them—that it wasn't his stupid hunt for Bigfoot.

By the time they reached the area where the ship was hidden, Henry had a stitch in his side that made it hard to breathe. He stumbled to a stop, bent double and wheezing. The sun had almost set, and the forest was dim.

"Henry." Vay's voice was tight and high.

He'd forgotten for a moment that Craig and Barbara hated Sadirians. They might attack Vay on sight.

She must be terrified. But she had come with him anyway, to help his new, very weird surrogate family. Even though she'd been trained to mistrust Lyrians, she was there for him.

And she had good reason to be afraid.

As she put her hand on his back, Barbara's booming voice came from above them.

"Get your hand off my nestling, Sadirian." Barbara

crashed to the ground in front of them, all four fists pounding into the earth, scattering the snow around her. "If you want to keep it attached to your arm."

Standing, she puffed out her chest. Henry hadn't noticed in the ship, but she was a good foot taller than Craig. And broader. All the spines on her body were standing straight out, quivering, which made her look even bigger—and a hell of a lot more menacing.

Henry managed to straighten himself and get between them. "This...is...Vay," he gasped. "She's...a friend."

"Sadirians don't have friends," Barbara said.

"They have...bondmates." His breath was finally slowing, though his heart still raced. "She's mine."

Barbara's eyebrow ridge rose, her mouth falling open— her mouth with its rows and rows of sharp teeth. It was a strangely human expression, especially considering her barely-humanoid countenance.

Gradually, the menace seeped back into her features. She closed her mouth, leaning forward and sniffing the air. Long, deep breaths. Then she pulled back and laughed.

"I should have smelled it on you," she said. She waved one of her arms at Vay dismissively. "Those uniforms make it difficult to perceive. Stars, Henry, how did you bond with a Sadirian? And why didn't you tell us before? We wouldn't have spoken so freely about them in front of you."

"I didn't know what she was," Henry said. "I just knew

that I loved her."

Barbara snorted at Vay, scowling.

"I love him, too," Vay said.

The corner of Barbara's mouth twitched. Not quite a smile, but it had taken an hour before she'd looked at Henry that way after they'd met.

"This is all happening really fast," Henry said. "Ridiculously fast. But we don't have time to…take our time."

"Nestling, you're not making sense."

"There's a Scorpiian in the area," he said. "It's been in my cabin. It can take my form."

He looked around, hoping that Craig would appear. Maybe jump down from a tree or just de-cloak himself and yell, "Surprise!" But Henry knew from the sick feeling in his stomach that neither of those would happen.

He closed his eyes briefly, taking a deep breath and letting it out.

"Barbara, where's Craig?"

Chapter Fifteen

Despite Vay's utter terror of the Lyrian a moment ago, now she felt nothing but sympathy. She couldn't imagine how she would feel if she faced a similar circumstance.

"He went for a walk shortly after you left." Barbara looked off in the direction of Henry's cabin.

Vay shook her head. "We didn't pass him on our way here. Is there a way you can track him?"

"He's my mate. Of course I can." She sniffed the air again, turning in a slow circle, then pointed. "This way."

Then she was off, and Vay's focus was on keeping up with her—and making sure Henry could as well. As the Lyrian—Barbara—pulled ahead, Vay realized they could just follow the giant trail Barbara was leaving behind in the snow.

"Don't we need...a plan or something?" Henry said, wheezing between the words. "Damn. I need...to work out more."

"I have a plan." Barbara looked back at Vay briefly over one of many shoulders. "You protect your mate. I'll protect mine."

Vay nodded, hope mingling with dread within her.

Barbara was accepting her. They would probably help Vay escape the Coalition—if they all survived this encounter. She was determined to make that happen.

"Go ahead," Henry said. "Vay, help her. I'll...catch up."

"It isn't much farther, nestling. The scent is getting stronger."

With that, Barbara vanished from sight. The trail she was making remained clear for a while longer, but then it stopped. A nearby tree shook, snow dropping to the ground beneath it.

Vay slowed down, then held out her arm to stop Henry. He bent over again, his breath fogging the air. He lifted the Lyrian scarf to his face to breathe through.

"We're close," she said.

"Whatever training they put you through, I need some of it."

She smiled, leaning in to kiss his cheek. "After we're through this and I'm free of the Coalition, I'd be happy to help you get in shape."

His eyes widened and he dropped the scarf away from his mouth. "You're going to ask them? You'll stay?"

"I don't know if I'll be able to stay on Earth, but I want to be with you."

He nodded. "We'll make it work. As soon as we save Craig."

She took his hand and pulled him along, following the signs of Barbara's passage through the trees. It didn't take long before they found another trail—the large tracks of a Lyrian walking with a smaller, human-sized being.

"It took my form," Henry said. "Craig's guard is down. He doesn't know it isn't me."

They quickened their pace again. Vay's wristband let out a warning buzz that she felt more than heard.

"Henry, my proximity sensor is going off."

"Proximity to what?" He kept moving forward, following the trail.

Vay grabbed his arm, but it was too late. She felt the tug of the gravity net just as Henry flew off his feet, pulling her with him. They hit the center of the energy web, hanging ten feet off the ground, unable to move.

"I don't see anything," Henry yelled. "What's holding us up?"

"A gravity net. The Scorpiian must have set traps."

There was a snowdrift below them. If she could deactivate the field, they shouldn't be hurt from the fall. But she had no way of reaching her wristband. And even if she could, she didn't know what to aim it at to destroy the field.

Lights flooded the trees around them, casting odd shadows on the ground as the sun finally set. One of the shadows moved toward them, long and spindly. She expected to see a Scorpiian—gray skin and huge black eyes. Instead, Henry stepped out from behind one of the trees.

Except not Henry.

"They'll throw anything in a uniform and call it a soldier these days," it said.

The hairs on the back of her neck stood on end. To hear an insult in the same soft voice that had whispered in her ear, had told her she was loved... She wanted to get away from it, but she was held fast.

"You're not even wearing your helmet." It shook its head. "Honestly, I'm tempted to just throw you back into the wild. 'Catch and release', as the Tau Ceti say. But you caught me at a bad time and I still need the human for bait."

It pulled a control disk from its pocket and tapped a few commands. Many of the trees around them vanished.

"Vay, what just happened?" the real Henry said.

"Holograms. Scorpiians deal in illusions and misperceptions."

"Right."

Instead of being deep in the forest, they were in a large clearing. A small shuttle was parked in the center of it, all jarring angles and odd isometric forms. For a species that could assume almost any form they wanted, the Scorpiians placed little value on appearances.

"Vay..."

She looked over at Henry. He was staring across the clearing, eyes glittering with unshed tears. She followed his gaze—and wished she hadn't.

A Lyrian was suspended between two massive trees. All of his arms and legs were pulled straight away from his body. His head listed against his shoulder, though, and his eyes were closed.

"Craig," Henry said.

The Scorpiian paced in front of them. "Where is the female?"

"Go to hell."

"Henry, don't." Antagonizing it would only get them both killed sooner. She didn't believe for a moment it would really let them go.

The Scorpiian shook its head, then lifted the disk again. It pressed another control, and this time a burst of silver energy shot out from it. One of the trees behind them exploded in a shower of heat and light.

"Sooner or later—and I'm betting on sooner—she'll show up and get caught in one of my traps. Nothing can run, leap, slither, or fly into this clearing. Trust me, I've thought of all the angles."

It was overconfident. Vay didn't even see a weapon on it—just the control disk in its hand.

She needed to distract the Scorpiian—to keep him talking while they figured out what to do. Barbara had to be close, and Vay had seen for herself that Lyrians weren't the berserk beasts the Coalition had always described. If Barbara was watching and coming up with a plan, Vay had to get her more time and information.

"I don't doubt it," Vay said. "With all the forms you've probably taken."

It shrugged. Its face matched Henry's, but the expression was completely wrong. Cold efficiency. Henry radiated warmth.

"You have the nets to catch things that just walk or run," Vay said. "And I'm guessing nothing's getting in from above either.

"You're stalling."

"I'm a cultural programmer. I'm interested in learning more about your ways, especially since you have a unique understanding of what different beings are like."

"Where is the female?" the Scorpiian said.

Vay ignored it. "What about burrowers? Lyrians have a lot of arms. They're big, but I bet they can dig pretty well."

He punched a few more commands into his control disk, then glanced at his ship.

His ship...

She looked around the clearing and didn't see anything big enough to create the kinds of energy fields he was describing. She doubted he would bother with setting up a portable cloaking generator. Scorpiians didn't usually stay in one place for long. Which meant everything was probably being controlled by his ship.

"So you didn't have that covered?" she said.

"Vay, maybe don't help the guy out?" Henry whispered.

"I don't really think *Barbara* could burrow into here." Vay said the Lyrian's name louder than the other words, hoping to draw her attention.

"Now I have a name," the Scorpiian said.

"You're welcome." Vay nodded toward the ship. "And you should also thank me for letting you know to add the seismic sensor to all the other traps *being generated by your ship.*"

A furrow appeared between the Scorpiian's eyebrows. She hoped he wouldn't pick up on her weird emphasis.

"Make this easier on everybody and tell me where she is." The Scorpiian started edging away from them, moving closer to Craig. It knew something was up. "Maybe I'll let you go with mind-wipes."

Vay heard a loud creaking noise, like the wind pushing against the trees. But the air was still.

She smiled, and said, "I think you'll be letting us go regardless."

One of the largest trees Vay had ever seen came crashing down through the clearing, landing right in the center of it. Barbara rode it down, holding on to the massive trunk with all four arms. It landed right on the Scorpiian's ship.

The gravity net failed. Vay and Henry fell to the ground, landing in the soft snow.

The Scorpiian was on the other side of the tree, its eyes wide as it held its hands up toward Barbara. If it tried to run, Barbara would pounce, and he was well inside her range of attack.

"I'm sure we can work out a deal," it said.

It looked at the sparking wreckage of its ship as Barbara rolled the giant tree trunk back and forth, crushing the vehicle further. Vay doubted the Scorpiian had a backup vessel. From the look on Barbara's face, she doubted he would need one soon.

"Take off my nestling's face before I do it for you," Barbara growled.

The Scorpiian immediately started to glow. Its features shifted, for a brief moment appearing as its natural form— all long limbs and gray skin, with huge black eyes. Then it thickened and changed, the glow fading until Vay was looking at...

"Eric?"

The Scorpiian ignored her. This was definitely the same one that Eric and Sorca had dealt with, though.

"I have resources." Its voice had deepened to match Eric's, as well. "This doesn't have to end in violence."

"No, it doesn't," Barbara said. She gestured toward Vay and Henry with one of her arms. "Find Craig."

Then she turned back to the Scorpiian, baring her teeth. "This doesn't *have* to end in violence. But it will."

The Scorpiian started to glow as it lifted its arms to fend off her attack just as Barbara pounced.

Vay might not have been a model soldier, but she knew

how to follow orders. She also knew that she did not want to see what was about to happen to that Scorpiian. She almost felt sorry for it.

"Come on." She grabbed Henry's hand and pulled him up. "We have to get to Craig and make sure he's all right."

Henry nodded, running behind her as they made their way around the clearing's edge. Craig had fallen as well when the gravity nets failed. He lay still in a pile of snow that was almost the same color as his fur.

"No, no, no…" Henry ran to Craig's side, tugging on one arm to try to roll him over. Craig was so heavy, he didn't budge.

Suddenly, the Lyrian shot up from the snow. "I'm awake."

Henry lost his balance, tumbling onto the ground. Which left the Lyrian blinking at Vay, looking disoriented.

"I'm his mate," she yelled.

Henry said, "She's with me," at the same time.

Craig shook his head, then ran his hand over his face. His skin turned purplish.

"I'm aware," he said. "Moons, don't remind me."

"Wait, how do you know?" Henry said.

Vay helped him to his feet. She was wondering the same thing.

"I followed you back to your cabin to make sure you were okay and saw you two through the window." Craig snorted and looked away. "I suppose you *are* an adult of your species, as you keep saying. A little young to be bonding, though. Nestlings grow up too fast."

He sniffed a little. Henry let out a laugh and then grabbed Craig in a huge—for an Earthling—hug. Craig laughed as well, wrapping all of his arms around Henry at once.

A horrific screech pierced the air.

"What the hell is that?" Henry said.

Craig stood, setting Henry down next to Vay. "That is the sound of a Lyrian female protecting her nestling."

An arc of silver liquid flew through the air above the twisted limbs of the oak tree in front of them. Something bounced along after it.

"Oh dear," Craig said. He reached out with one set of hands and covered Henry's eyes, and then, to Vay's utter shock, he used his other set to cover her eyes. "Barbara, if you could shut off the lights… There are children present."

There was another screech, then a lot of banging, and the lights went dead.

"Thank you," Craig sang out. "I think she's going to be a while. Let's head to our ship while she finishes up."

"Yeah," Henry said. "Let's…do that."

Chapter Sixteen

Back at the ship, sipping a warm cup of something Henry couldn't identify, he tried to make sense of the last day. Bigfoot was real—and an alien. With an incredibly violent and protective mate. He'd been adopted by them, which was apparently part of their cultural norms. And he was kinda-sorta married to Vay.

Mated, bonded, whatever they wanted to call it.

It was amazing. His life was amazing, and he had a feeling it was only going to become more so.

"And then he said, 'It means I'm hungry'." Craig let out a huge laugh, regaling Vay with the one and only embarrassing story he had to tell about Henry.

Some things about parenting were universal, it seemed.

She laughed along with Craig, casting a warm smile Henry's way. The only thing missing was Barbara. Craig had said she would be fine, but Henry still worried.

As if on cue, the door to the ship whooshed open and she stomped in. Silver liquid was dripping from her fur.

"Darling, if you're going to shake, do it in the other room," Craig said. "I don't want you getting quicksilver on the kids."

She growled, then stomped past them.

"Where's the Scorpiian?" Henry couldn't help himself. That was a lot of...Scorpiian blood? He knew from the sounds of what was happening back at the clearing that it was very probably dead, but he had to be sure.

Barbara paused, then turned to face him. She grinned, again showing Henry all of those sharp, sharp teeth.

In a rumbling voice that was almost a purr, she said, "Which part?"

Craig stepped up behind her, nudging her through the door to the other room. "Let's leave it at that."

"Yeah, that sounds like a good idea," Henry said.

When Barbara was gone, Craig turned to Vay, picking up a lock of her hair between his fingers and cocking his head to the side as he examined it. Henry was glad to see that she didn't flinch away.

"So, my new Sadirian kin, what will happen next?" Craig let go of her hair, then crossed the small room and sat on a stack of crates marked "C. Addison". Henry wondered if that was the name of one of Craig and Barbara's "open-minded human contacts".

Vay glanced at Henry and he nodded in what he hoped was a reassuring manner.

"Well, Henry and I had talked about me leaving the Coalition, but I'm not sure that's for the best."

He felt like the floor had suddenly fallen out from under him. Did she not want to be with him after all?

"I didn't realize you'd changed your mind," he said.

"I didn't." She reached over and grasped his hand. "I want to be with you. And I want both of us to be able to stay on your homeworld. But with Scorpiians and Tau Ceti and Centaurans on Earth—"

"And about half a dozen more sentient species that we know of," Craig said.

Vay cast a quick glare at him. "Earth is in a very dangerous position. It might actually become part of the Coalition before long."

"Stars guide us away from that path," Craig said.

Barbara entered the room, her fur white and clean again. She sat next to Craig and hooked her leg with his, planting one set of hands on her thighs and crossing her other arms across her chest.

"What are you suggesting, Sadirian?" she said.

"Vay." Henry squeezed Vay's hand. "Her name is Vay."

Barbara snorted. He knew by now that was a good sign.

Vay turned toward Henry. "You said you wanted to join the Department of Homeworld Security. Did you mean it?"

At the time, it had been a joke. Mostly. But there was a grain of truth in it. He was definitely interested.

"Yes."

"And do you still want to, even after everything you've learned and seen?" she said.

"More than ever."

She leaned forward and kissed him, and for that moment, he forgot everything else—Scorpiians and Lyrians and evil space empires and aliens—and it was just him and Vay and the warmth and love between them.

Until Craig cleared his throat. "Children."

Vay pulled back, still smiling broadly, and turned toward the Lyrians.

"You've adopted Henry," Vay said. She turned to Henry and gave him one of those amazing smiles. "And Henry has bonded with me."

"That's fairly clear," Barbara said.

"The law is also clear in this matter," she said. "The formalities will take me forever, but if we follow proper protocols, which are really common sense—don't let other Earthlings know aliens are real or especially that we're on Earth, don't let any of our technology fall into the wrong hands—I can have us classified as a family with an Earth connection. We'll all be allowed to stay or go as we wish. It'll take time—and a lot of authorizations, but I really think I can make it happen."

Barbara kept glaring. Her mouth started to twitch. The twitch spread until her lips were pulled in a huge smile. Then she threw her head back and laughed.

Craig had his eyes covered and was shaking his head, but his body trembled with laughter. "Stars, Sadirians are hilarious. They make all of these rules and laws to control the universe."

Barbara finally stopped laughing, but her grin remained huge. "If we can use those laws to our advantage, we're all for it."

"And more importantly, it will let us keep our family together." Craig nudged her with a shoulder.

"Of course, sweetheart." She leaned closer, until their ears touched and started...caressing each other.

"I'm beginning to understand those kids who aren't comfortable with their parents being overly affectionate," Henry said.

Both Lyrians turned to him and grinned, but this time, the look was downright diabolical.

"We have many arms," Barbara said.

"And we are fond of hugs," Craig added.

The room wasn't that big, so when they reached across and grabbed Henry and Vay, there was nowhere to run, even if he'd wanted to. But as they pulled them both into the biggest, furriest hug he'd ever felt, he *didn't* want to run. He finally felt like he was home.

Epilogue

Every trudging step was agony. The snow around Zemanni's feet sizzled and melted, little puffs of steam rising from his footprints.

Almost there.

Henry's cabin had melted into the rest of the forest in Zemanni's blurred vision. Only the little lights that the human had strung over the structure helped Zemanni pick it out from the brown and white background of the wintry trees.

Sweat ran into his eyes. Human sweat.

What's happening to me?

He fell against the door, the cold wood heating against his fevered skin. Even if he survived the intensely high body temperatures cycling through his system, he would eventually succumb to the cold if he didn't get covered.

The group who had nearly killed him had headed in the direction of the Lyrians' spacecraft while Zemanni began the agonizing process of pulling his body back together from the pieces Barbara had torn him into. He'd lost so much of his quicksilver. Almost all of it. And now he was trapped.

But not for long.

He fumbled with the handle of the door, knowing Henry kept it unlocked. Stumbling into the cabin as the door opened, Zemanni veered toward Henry's closet.

Clothes. He needed to find clothes that would fit him. And then he needed to find a base of operations where he could regain his strength and figure out the logistics of his next move—obtain more quicksilver and purge his system of this alien DNA that was infecting him.

He paused by a small mirror that hung on the wall, staring at the reflection that wasn't really his.

"Eric Peterson," Zemanni growled, as if the DNA matrix could hear him. The *human* DNA that was changing him in ways he didn't understand. But he did understand one thing with a certainty that he felt in his bizarrely stiff human bones.

This was not the end for him.

—

I'll let you all in on a secret. I originally planned to kill off the Scorpiian assassin in *Tied up in Customs*, but he was too fascinating for me to let go of that easily. Of course, I realized the best way to get to know him better was to give him his own book. And thus, the sixth book in *The Department of Homeworld Security* was born! Read on for a sneak peek of *Duration of Stay!*

Duration of Stay

The Department of Homeworld Security
Book Six

Chapter One

The windows of Brooke's car were covered in fog. If she'd been sitting inside—maybe drinking one of the gazillion hot drinks she'd made for customers that day—it would make sense. But she was just getting off her shift, and her car had been parked in the nearly empty lot for hours.

"Elliot, you asshole," Brooke said. "Get out of my car and give me back my spare key."

Not that he'd need it to get in later. He knew that the

back driver's side door didn't lock right anymore. She lined up her keys between her fingers, making sure the sharp edges pointed out like claws. He'd only been incredibly annoying since the breakup, but she wanted to be ready in case he'd finally gone off the deep end.

She jerked open the door and let out a disgusted grunt. He was lying sort of curled up in the footwell, his dark hair masking his face.

"Seriously, this is reaching entirely new levels of pathetic. It's been three months. Get over it."

A sudden feeling of misgiving shivered through her. Had he cut his hair? And had he always been that tall? And buff?

Her car was a piece of crap, but it was spacious. And he was suddenly taking up every inch of the available space.

His legs were bent and he was hunched over with his arms wrapped around his torso. Her skin felt electrified as she realized that whoever this guy sleeping in the back seat of her car was, he wasn't Elliot.

She raised her key-studded hand. "What are you doing in my car?"

The man lifted his head and turned to look at her. Her heart thudded in her chest.

His dark hair was a little longer at the front, dusting across his forehead. It was short in the back—nothing getting in the way of her view of his shoulders, which were massive. He had a long, straight nose, perfectly curved lips, honey-brown eyes, and an angular jaw covered in a thick coat of stubble. He was absolutely gorgeous.

The sweat coating his skin glistened faintly in the dim light. Why was he sweating when all he had on was a pair of jeans and a flannel shirt? He wasn't even wearing shoes.

She lowered her arm and stepped forward, poking her head into the back seat of her car. "Are you okay?"

He was shaking violently, his whole body trembling. He held up a hand to her and his sleeve fell back enough for her to see his corded forearm—and the line of silver light circling it. His skin was *glowing*.

"I won't hurt you," he said.

His voice sent a frisson through her. It was deep and strong, even with the obvious strain in it. Who the heck was this guy? *What* was he?

"You need help," she said.

"No doctors."

"Duh."

She slammed the door and quickly climbed into the driver's seat. It took several tries, but her decrepit car finally started. She had almost walked that morning, but it was too cold even for the couple of blocks between her home and work. Before putting the car in gear, she looked over the bench seat into the back.

"Do you promise you won't try to eat my face off?" she

said.

"I won't try to eat your face off." He looked vaguely insulted at the idea. The furrows between his eyebrows deepened.

Crap, even his forehead was sexy. How was that possible?

"Or anything else?" she asked.

"I'm not going to eat you." This time, there was definite frustration in his tone.

"Okay."

She turned back around and took a deep breath, then exhaled. This was like something out of a movie. Hopefully not a horror flick.

As she pulled out of the parking lot, she said, "So what are you? A ghost? Fallen angel?"

"Scorpiian."

"What, like a bug?"

"I'm from Scorpii-2."

"Is that a company or something? Are you an android?" The silver glow could be some kind of LEDs in his body.

He let out a frustrated grunt. "It's a planet in the Scorpii system."

"Oh my God. You're an alien."

"Yeah."

An alien. In the back seat of her car.

"Are you having some kind of allergic reaction to our planet?"

"What? Why would I…"

"No offense, but you don't look so good."

She turned into the parking lot for her apartment complex. Luckily, there was a spot right next to the stairs up to her apartment. At midday in the middle of the week, no one was around.

"I mean, you look hot," she said. "But you also look… hot."

"Thanks for clarifying."

She ignored the crack, though she was glad to know he understood sarcasm. That would make it easier to communicate.

"Are you supposed to glow like that?" she said.

"No." He let out a groan and she heard him shift around more.

"Crap, you're not dying, are you?"

She set the parking brake, but didn't turn off the engine. She understood his desire to avoid any organization that might stuff him in a lab and experiment on him, but if it was a choice between that or death, he might have to reconsider the whole "no doctors" thing.

"I'm not dying. I'm acclimating."

"So it *is* some kind of reaction."

He let out another frustrated sigh. It was easier to handle than the little pain noise he'd made.

She stepped out into the frigid air, keeping her apartment key ready and wondering how she was going to get him up the stairs.

"Mom always said I was a rescuer," Brooke murmured. "If she could see me now."

The alien had managed to get himself out of the footwell and onto the back seat. He was dragging himself across the bench toward her. She opened his door and reached in to help him. His skin was burning hot.

"You have a fever," she said.

"I'm acclimating."

"Right. Whatever." She draped his arm over her shoulder and shut both car doors. "Let's go."

He started to pull away from her, veering toward the mound of snow piled at the edge of the lot. "I need to lower my body temperature."

"If someone sees you lying in a pile of snow, they'll call the cops."

Especially since he was still glowing. She could see more lines now that he was up—soft silver light gleaming around his neck, shoulders, and arms. There were even dim circles around his thighs that she could see faintly through his jeans.

He let her take the lead, though he stumbled a few times. It seemed like he was mostly able to support his own weight, which was helpful. All that muscle would make him way too heavy for her to drag up the stairs. They made it up to her apartment without drawing any attention, and she unlocked the door and helped him inside.

She slid the deadbolts and chain into place, just in case Elliot decided to show up unannounced—again. He needed to give her back her damned spare keys. If he walked in on Brooke while another guy was there... She didn't have the energy to handle the tantrum he'd throw.

She led the alien hottie further into her place. "The bathroom's over here."

"My body doesn't eliminate waste the way human bodies do," he said.

"Ew, really? Do you eat?"

He didn't answer her, probably because his body had started trembling violently again. If lowering his body temperature was necessary, they needed to get on that right away.

There were a lot of ways she'd like to get on his body, alien or not.

She dragged her attention back to the task at hand, pushing the other thoughts away. She was supposed to be helping the poor guy, not drooling over him. She kicked open the door to the bathroom.

"We need to get you in the tub. I can get snow from outside to help you cool down." She leaned him against a wall, then plugged the drain and started the cold water running.

When she turned back to him, he'd already unbuttoned his shirt. He was even more built than she'd thought. His chest was broad, without an ounce of extra fat. His abdomen rippled with muscle, and dark hair cascaded down his chest and belly, disappearing into his jeans.

"I'm trapped in this human form," he said.

"I can think of worse fates than being trapped in *this* one."

His shirt tangled around his arms as he tried to pull it off. He leaned heavily against the wall, as if just unbuttoning it had exhausted him. Lines of silver traced down the chiseled muscles of his abdomen, but they weren't smooth, as she'd thought earlier. They were jagged, almost like scars. But if they were scars, it looked like he'd been torn limb from limb and reassembled.

"Vapor pits," he said.

She shook her head. "I don't understand. Do you need some vapor pits or something?" Not that she had any idea what that was.

"It's a..." He let out an aggravated grunt. "I'm angry."

"Oh, it's a swear." When he stared at her blankly, she said, "Next time, try, 'fuck' or 'dammit'."

He glared at her, then tugged at his shirt.

"Let me help you." She peeled the shirt down the knotted muscle of his arms and then tossed it aside. As he braced himself against the wall, she reached around and unfastened his jeans.

"Normally, I can just form whatever clothing I need," he said. "This external material is impossible to manage."

"So, you're some kind of shapeshifting alien?"

He grunted. It wasn't a denial.

"You picked a good look."

She tugged his jeans past an ass that could be put on display in a museum, then dragged them over legs that surpassed her wildest fantasies. He had just the right amount of hair covering his perfectly sculpted thighs and toned calves.

He stepped into the water as soon as he was free of his clothes, then slid down the wall. He let out a sigh as he sank into the water's chilly embrace, not bothering to try to cover himself.

The dark hair on his chest continued in a trail that led to the thicker triangle around his dick. The water was freezing. Wasn't that all supposed to *shrink* in the cold?

Wow...

Not lusting after him was going to be a hell of a lot harder than she thought.

—

About the Author

USA Today Bestselling author Cassandra Chandler uses her vivid imagination to make the world more interesting, spawning the ideas she turns into her whimsical Science Fiction romcoms and darkly evocative Paranormal and Urban Fantasy Romances. Fast-paced and funny, lighthearted or dark, her stories will introduce you to characters you want to be friends with and worlds where you'd like to build a vacation home.

www.ingramcontent.com/pod-product-compliance
Lightning Source LLC
Chambersburg PA
CBHW051242170626
46809CB00004B/1449